BABY, IT'S H

The winter wind was howling and Catherine was violently shivering when she came to Skye at night. He found out why she was so cold after his hand roved over the cloth of her dress until he could draw up the hem and reach under it. Not only wasn't Catherine wearing a cape over the dress, she also wasn't wearing anything underneath.

But Skye stopped worrying about her physical state when she let his hand explore her secret flesh.

And the Trailsman's last doubts fled when she eagerly reached for him. Catherine might have started out a mite cold, but she sure as hell wasn't frigid. . . .

Exciting Westerns by Jon Sharpe from SIGNET

THE
WHITE HELL
TRAIL

by

Jon Sharpe

A SIGNET BOOK

NEW AMERICAN LIBRARY

PUBLISHER'S NOTE

This novel is a work of fiction. Names, characters, places, and incidents either are the product of the author's imagination or are used fictitiously, and any resemblance to actual persons, living or dead, events, or locales is entirely coincidental.

The first chapter of this book previously appeared in *Six-Gun Salvation*, the forty-seventh volume in this series.

The Trailsman

Beginnings . . . they bend the tree and they mark the man. Skye Fargo was born when he was eighteen. Terror was his midwife, vengeance his first cry. Killing spawned Skye Fargo, ruthless, cold-blooded murder. Out of the acrid smoke of gunpowder still hanging in the air, he rose, cried out a promise never forgotten.

The Trailsman, they began to call him, all across the West: searcher, scout, hunter, the man who could see where others only looked, his skills for hire but not his soul, the man who lived each day to the fullest, yet trailed each tomorrow. Skye Fargo, the Trailsman, the seeker who could take the wildness of a land and the wanting of a woman and make them his own.

*1861 . . . Taos Pueblo,
northern New Mexico Territory*

1

The Trailsman stiffened when the ratty-looking blond man entered the cantina. Fargo had been relaxed—as relaxed as he ever permitted himself to be, anyway, which was still more vigilant and attentive than most men when they were trying to remain alert—with a drink in one hand and the warm, slim waist of a mestizo girl under the other. Now he drew himself erect, his whipcord frame taut under a rush of sudden tension. He set the glass aside and his other hand fell unconsciously away from the now-forgotten girl. His lake-blue eyes went suddenly cold. There was ice in the look he gave the newcomer.

The girl, affronted, tried to snuggle back against him. Then she saw the look that had come into those coldly flashing eyes. Her hand went to her throat in a gasp of quick fear, and she scuttled away—away from the sense of raw danger that now surrounded this tall, darkly handsome gringo with the lank black hair and the ready laughter.

Fargo was not even aware of her as she left him. His concentration was total. It was focused solely on the man with the scraggly whiskers and too-long-uncut-and-unwashed blond hair.

°"Howdy, Adam," someone said, making room for the newcomer at the bar.

The name was a confirmation. But Fargo needed no confirmation.

This was the man he had been seeking. For all the tortured years.

This man was one of them. He had to be.

One of those who had come by stealth to kill and maim and destroy. One of those who had wiped out a family—Skye Fargo's family—and lived to become the object of a vow that Fargo raged to the heavens when he discovered the bodies of the only people in the world he truly loved.

And now here the man was. His death would be the culmination of that vow.

Adam Brighton. It was not the name he had been born with. It was not the name he had used that horror-ridden day. But it was one he had used before and now made the mistake of adopting again.

Fargo's jaw muscles clenched so tightly he couldn't swallow. His arms and shoulders ached from strain. Yet to anyone standing more than a pace distant he would have seemed calm, even outwardly casual, as he took a slow step forward and then another.

The Colt rode at his waist. His hand slid closer to the use-worn butt.

Fargo moved up behind the man who called himself Brighton. He stopped five paces away. Brighton was laughing at something one of his friends had said. He was picking up a mug of foaming native beer.

"Adam Brighton." Fargo's voice rang cold and crisp through the din of many conversations. The cantina fell silent for less than a second, then there was the clatter of falling chairs as men scrambled out of the way. The icy timbre of Fargo's voice was all too easily recognized as a challenge.

The man who called himself Brighton turned. His face, burned by sun and wind, went suddenly pale.

"I heard you were here," Fargo said. "You talked too much in Mora, Brighton. You let them know where you were heading. Now it's time to pay the piper, Brighton."

Brighton began to tremble. A tic fluttered in the corner of his right eye, and his hands were shaky. "I don't know you," he wailed.

"No, you don't," Fargo said agreeably. "But I know you. I've been following you a long time. Now I've found you."

"My . . . you're lookin' for a man named Brighton, mister. That ain't really my name. I swear it ain't."

Fargo's lips parted in a frightening caricature of a smile. "I know," he whispered. His eyes were cruel now.

"I made a mistake," the man who called himself Brighton quavered. "I know that now, mister. I learned my lesson. I swear that to you. I wouldn't do it again. Not never."

Fargo barked sharply, a sound that might have been intended as laughter although there was no hint of humor in the bitterness of it. "I know you won't, Brighton," he said.

"Look here, mister," a man standing near Brighton protested. "You cain't do this. The fella made himself a mistake. Hell, man, we all of us make mistakes."

Fargo turned to the stranger. "What I hear is that you're backing him. Is that what you want?"

The friend looked from Fargo to Brighton and back again. For a moment his courage held. But only for a moment. He looked into the tall man's icy-blue eyes. "No," he mumbled. He turned and slipped away into the crowd that had gathered along the side walls of the cantina.

"Well?" Fargo asked

"I'm beggin' you, mister. Let me go back and serve my time. I'll confess. I swear I will. I won't give you no trouble. You can have the reward."

Reward. As if any amount of money could ever repay Fargo for the losses he had suffered.

How much money would compensate a young man for the loss of the father who had taught him? For the mother who had birthed and suckled him? For the younger brother whose admiration had been embarrassingly, and so often annoyingly, close to worship?

What kind of reward money could wipe out those losses? Fargo wondered bitterly.

Hell, Fargo didn't even know what else this son of a bitch might be wanted for. He didn't care. What he cared about was that this man paid for the loss of Fargo's family.

The man who called himself Brighton must have seen Fargo's answer in his eyes. Brighton shook all the harder. His mouth worked, but no sounds passed through his lips. He was facing the specter of implacable death. And he knew it.

Fargo stared at him. All the years, all the countless trails, were behind him now. Forgotten.

All he could think of was the gunpowder stink in the place that had once been a happy home. His nostrils were filled with the remembered odors of gunsmoke and fresh blood.

He stared at the man and remembered all of it.

So many times, beside so many campfires, he had looked forward to this moment. It was almost as if Skye Fargo had already lived through this moment ten thousand times before.

Brighton was standing there with a revolver at his belt. Fargo studied him intently. There was a bald spot on the back of the man's head Fargo could not see because of his hat. But he knew it was there.

There would be a scar under that filthy shirt. Fargo had been told about that scar. The dimpled pucker of a long-ago bullet. Someone had shot the man once, nearly killed him. Fargo did not know but had always secretly hoped that it was his father who had holed the son of a bitch.

Fargo sensed the movement before he saw it, and he turned in time to see Brighton's friend, in a surge of courage, swinging a chair at him.

The Trailsman ducked, the chair glancing the top of his head. The blow was not serious, but it caused him to lose his balance and he went sprawling across the floor. He lay on his back looking into the barrel of Brighton's revolver.

Brighton was peering down at him nervously, his thumb fumbling at the spur of the hammer. "You ain't takin' me back now, mister."

Fargo took a chance. He kicked the chair he'd been hit with and that now lay at his feet. The momentary distraction was all he needed as he pulled the Colt from his holster and aimed it at the blond man standing over him.

The big Colt bellowed, the force of the exploding gunpowder rocking the use-polished walnut grips into the web of Fargo's fist.

Flame and smoke and superheated lead spat from the muzzle. The heavy pellet of hot lead smashed into Adam Brighton's belly.

Brighton staggered. His mouth gaped open in shock and pain, and he doubled over, the Remington in his hand forgotten. The revolver fell from suddenly nerveless fingers. It hit the floor muzzle down, the impact tripping the hammer and causing the gun to discharge. The force of the unintended explosion sent the revolver dancing crazily into the air.

Brighton went down. He lay on the floor, hunched into himself with both hands clasped to his shattered gut.

"Jesus," someone murmured. "So fast. . . ."

Brighton moaned. The Remington lay beside him.

Fargo stepped forward and used the side of his boot to sweep the Remington out of reach.

The man who called himself Adam Brighton was dying. He lay on the floor and looked up at his killer with pain-racked eyes. His lips moved. He had to try three times to get the single word out, and when it did come, there was a trickle of blood that accompanied it.

"Why?"

"You ask me that? You know why." Fargo knelt beside Brighton, his expression as hard as a face carved in stone.

For the first time in years he softly spoke the name that once had been his, the name he had carried from his birth until the time of his rebirth, until he took the name Fargo as a reminder of the father who had died because of his employment by Wells Fargo.

Brighton looked at Fargo blankly. "Never . . . never kilt them, mister. Never even heard of them." He gasped, then shuddered as his eyes began to glaze.

"Shit"

Fargo felt a numbness spreading inside him now, replacing the fury that had been driving him.

He reached forward and swept Brighton's hat off his head. Brighton's hair was full and thick. There was no bald patch.

Fargo rolled Brighton onto his back and ripped his shirt open. Looking for the scar that *had* to be there. There was no scar.

"No!" Fargo cried out. He rose to his feet, turned and stumbled blindly away.

The alias. The description. The hatred. They had all been accurate. They had been right.

He had come to Taos in search of the man who called himself Adam Brighton. He had been forced to kill him. But he would've killed him anyway, Fargo knew. And he had been the wrong man. The man who had helped to slaughter Fargo's family still walked free and cocky in the world.

There was the bitter taste of bile in Fargo's throat. He felt suddenly worn and sluggish.

He stumbled to the bar and groped on its surface for a glass someone had left there. He raised the glass to his lips and tossed it down without tasting the fiery burn of it.

He saw the girl who had been with him before, reached for her wrist and grasped it in the hard grip of his hand.

She looked frightened, but he did not see. Still holding onto her, he walked blindly from the cantina into the cold of the winter's night and was not aware when it became she who began to lead him.

She took him around behind the cantina to a line of daub and wattle jacales. They had been built within sight of the tall, walled pueblo that once had been the focus of Taos' existence.

She took him inside and wrapped her arms around this handsome, trembling *yanqui*. Instinct replaced reason, and her instinct was to give comfort to the big, black-haired, suddenly unsure American.

She pressed him down onto her cot and left him for a moment to drape the low doorway with a blanket, keeping out the cold and the curious.

When she returned to him, she lay beside him, pressing the warmth of her body against him, trying to give him comfort in the only way she knew how.

They shared no common language, this dark man and she, but none was needed.

Deft fingers stripped his clothing away and then her own. Naked, she covered him with blankets and crawled under the coverings at his side, pressing herself against him.

His body was hard. He bore old scars on his flesh. He bore new ones, she knew, in his heart.

She took him in her hands, her touch bringing forth the arousal of his animal maleness.

He grew hard under her touch, and she smiled to herself at the size and strength of him there.

He listened as she spoke to him softly in her own tongue. He didn't understand, but it didn't matter.

The softness of her words and the heat of her touch were enough.

She draped a full thigh over his legs, pressing against him, and raised herself to cover and straddle him. She smiled and reached down between his belly and hers to guide him into position. Then she lowered herself onto him, impaling herself on the spear of his manhood.

Her eyes, a soft and liquid brown, widened with pleasure as she filled herself with him.

Skye Fargo's eyes slowly regained their focus, and he became aware of where and what he was.

His hands reached for her, with purpose as he felt the slim planes of her back, the warmth and texture of her dusky skin. His hands slid around to the front to cup one soft breast and then the other.

He found her nipples, large and very dark, and rolled them between thumb and forefinger. The girl moaned and began to move her hips, providing the impetus that he still lacked.

Fargo sighed and pulled her down closer so he could take one nipple and then the other between his lips. He nipped lightly at them, and they became harder, elongating slightly in response to him. She moaned again and began to move faster and more insistently.

"Yes," Fargo whispered. It was the first he had spoken since the shock of the discovery, and she was glad for it. Without understanding the reasons for his behavior, she knew that he was wounded somewhere deep inside his soul.

Fargo pulled her down against his chest and wrapped his arms around her, holding her very tight for long minutes, not allowing her to move. Then, he took command of her.

He held her to him and rolled over so that he was on top of her, still socketed deep within the heat of her body. He nuzzled the sensitive hollow at the side of her neck and began to pump slowly and gently in and out.

She opened herself to him, welcoming the growing intensity of his thrusts, knowing without words that this was necessary and good.

Fargo raised himself from her far enough that he could see her eyes. She looked into them deeply, blue eyes—warm and alive once again—probing into her own brown ones, and she smiled.

Fargo smiled back at her and bent to kiss her. The soft mounds of her breasts were warm against him. The grip of her thighs was tight around him. And the pull of her sex surrounding his shaft was hot and welcoming.

"Thank you," he said, knowing that she would understand the sound if not the words.

She said something to him in a language that was not Spanish, then began to move, raising her body to him and falling away again.

Fargo began to respond to her stroking, assuming control now and thrusting with deep, powerful, demanding plunges.

He watched and felt with pleasure as her breath quickened and her gaze became remote, turning inward and concentrating on the sensations that were building inside her loins.

There was a matching rise of pleasurable pressure in him, and he mated his pace and his responses to hers, waiting for her to build with him.

The speed of their coupling quickened. His breathing came faster and faster, and the sweat from his chest gathered warm and slick between her breasts.

He pumped furiously into her now. She clutched frantically with her arms, and quivering thighs bucked beneath him, seeking to draw ever more of him into herself.

Her eyes closed and she bit at her underlip with white, small teeth as her head arched backward until the sinews at her throat stood out sharply under the brown skin.

"Aieee!"

She shuddered and stiffened beneath him, and Fargo let go of his control, allowing the hot, joyous fluids to gush and spew from his body deep into hers.

Fargo trembled slightly from the intensity of it. Then he collapsed onto her, exhausted, drained more from spent emotions than from the joining of man with woman.

He lay there, panting, feeling the sweat trickle from his armpits to drop onto her body.

Eventually he rolled off her, but held her close, drawing comfort from the nearness of her and the feel of her flesh against his.

And eventually his hand crept out to tangle his fingers in the dark, curling bush of her pubic hair.

This time the impetus and the desire were his, and the girl smiled as she opened herself to receive him again.

"You're Fargo? The one they call the Trailsman?"

Fargo looked up from his breakfast and nodded. The man standing over the table was of middle age and medium height. There was nothing else about him, though, that was at all average. He had a look of tough, trouble-weathered competence, and a stubby, sawed-off percussion shotgun with exceptionally large bores dangled from his left hand. The Trailsman found himself wishing he knew if this man was left- or right-handed.

"I am," he said calmly.

The man pulled his coat back a few inches to expose a brass star pinned to his shirt pocket. "Sam Bowen," he said. "Territorial marshal. Mind if I sit?"

Fargo motioned toward the chair across from him. He was rather pleased to note that Bowen laid the shotgun aside when he sat down. A squat, greasy-looking waiter had coffee in front of Bowen almost before the man's butt touched the chair bottom. It was a small thing, but Fargo made note of it. Sam Bowen was not only known here, he was respected and quite probably feared by the locals.

Bowen put his left hand on top of the table in full view and picked up his coffeecup with his right. He smiled.

"I went through my flyers this morning. There's two rewards you can collect on William Dolan Faye, the man you killed last night. He was a deserter and a bank robber. So you're due fifty dollars from the government for collecting a deserter. That's standard. The other's a hundred from the bank at Larned. Seems he shot a teller. I need to know do you want the money sent here or forwarded someplace else."

The taste of bile rose in Fargo's throat, conflicting with the spices of his meal. "I don't want it," he said.

Bowen's eyebrows went up. "You're so damn rich you turn down that kind of money?"

"I was forced to shoot Faye, but I would've done it anyway, I admit. But not for money, that's for damn sure. It had to do with something else. Unfortunate for Billy Faye, I made a mistake." Fargo sighed. He was no longer interested in eating. "You know any poor folks around Taos?"

"That's a damn-fool question, Fargo. Most of the folks around here don't know where their next bean is coming from."

"Give the money to them, then. I don't want it."

The lawman nodded. He made a motion as if to leave the table, then thought better of it and sank back down onto the chair. "I don't suppose you'd be looking for work?" he asked.

"It depends. Some things I don't hire out for."

"This is a guiding job. You lead the way and keep the party in meat."

Fargo shrugged.

"I might as well tell you, nobody else in Taos wants the job."

Fargo's interest was piqued. His expression showed it.

"Guides we got by the shitpotful down here. Hell, there's been comings and goings between Taos and the beaver country up north for the past forty years. But that's the direction these folks want to go, north, and the Indians over in the pueblo say there's a helluva storm brewing. They're shaking rattles and stomping in circles and telling everybody to pull in for the next full month. Personally, I think all this incantation stuff is a load of shit, but none of the locals are willing to go out."

Skye Fargo didn't share that opinion, possibly because of his one-quarter Indian blood. On the other hand, he was close to being broke. And there was damned little that would make him back away from a challenge. Especially since right now he was anxious to get the hell out of Taos Pueblo.

"This party can pay?"

"They're offering a hundred dollars a day to get them up to a mining camp called Leadville. You know it?"

"I've been there. Hell, it's only four days from here."

"Something like that."

"At a hundred a day?"

"That's what they've been waving at the locals. Up to you if you think you can do better."

Fargo grinned. "The Queen of England probably doesn't make a hundred a day."

"Should I tell them you are interested?"

Fargo nodded.

Bowen stood, turned. He paused and turned back to extend his hand, which Fargo shook.

"What was that for?"

Bowen shrugged. "It might not mean that much to you, Trailsman. But there will be some hungry kids make it through the winter around here because of that money you don't want."

The territorial marshal picked up his short, ugly scattergun and walked away. Fargo watched him go and was damned glad that Marshal Sam Bowen didn't have it in for him.

"You come highly recommended," the dapper little man said. "*Very* highly."

Fargo shrugged. Apparently, Sam Bowen had been lavish in his praises of the Trailsman.

"My name is Amon Porter, Mr. Fargo," the aging dandy went on. "I am the road manager, and indeed the owner, of the Porter Players, a traveling troupe of exceptionally gifted, I might add exceptionally talented Shakespearean and contemporary, uh, entertainers.'' He smiled modestly, as if he fully expected that the world would surely recognize the name.

Fargo gave Amon Porter another looking-over. His scant experience with traveling road shows had been that most of them were a bunch of chronically broke has-beens and never-would-bes.

Amon Porter, on the other hand, certainly looked to be prosperous enough. He wore a very nicely tailored suit, yellow vest with matching spats, and a gaudy bauble in his stickpin that would have bought out every girl in Aunt Maidie's Pleasure Palace for the next year and a half.

"How many in your party?'' Fargo asked

"Five, including myself,'' Porter said.

"You provide all the supplies?''

"Of course. And we shall agree to pay you in advance for the first five days of your employment.''

"It generally only takes four days to get from here to Leadville.''

"The fifth day's wage will be considered a bonus if you can get us to the community on time, Mr. Fargo.''

"Generous of you.''

"Not at all, sir. You see, our arrival in that desolate mining camp may have no significance to you, sir, but it is vitally important to us. Aside from the fact that we have a booking there, an investor in one of the major mining properties of the camp is also an extremely wealthy and extremely influential backer of, uh, theatrical endeavors. It is of paramount importance that we reach the camp and begin our performances there before this gentleman returns East, as he is certainly apt to do if the local soothsayers are correct in their predictions of a difficult winter. Our appearance in Leadville at the earliest opportunity, sir, could quite frankly be our breakthrough to the legitimate theaters of New York and Boston. It could very well spell the difference between moderate success and glowing tribute—with, of course, the fortune that accompanies such fame in our chosen field.''

"I see," Fargo said. He did understand, more or less, but the truth was that he didn't really give a damn why the Porter Players wanted to reach Leadville. The fact that they were willing to pay him five hundred dollars for four days' work was quite enough. "Couple things you got to get straight, Porter," he said.

"Yes?"

"Once we start moving, I'm in charge. Whatever I say goes on the trail. I won't take the job any other way."

"Agreed," Porter said.

"One other thing. I assume, if you're like most of the road outfits, you got you a fancy painted wagon that you roll your show in."

"Of course."

"Leave it here."

"What?"

"I said you have to leave it here. A lot of folks—white ones especially—say these wrinkled-up blanket Indians are full of shit when they make a prediction. Me, I've seen them be right too many times to turn up my nose when they say something. If they're right—and I'm not saying they are, only that I want to be prepared in case of it—I can get you through with pack animals but not with a pretty and conspicuous wagon. Not over Poncha Pass in a snowstorm, I can't. So if getting through interests you, then I suggest you leave the wagon here and go with pack animals for whatever you've got to carry."

"All right," the little man agreed. There was no hesitation whatsoever in his reply.

Fargo had expected an argument, at least a desire that the man be convinced. But he didn't pause for a second before acceding to the Trailsman's demand.

"Can we leave today?" Porter asked.

"You think you can unload your wagon and round up mules before dark?"

Porter smiled. "Give me an hour, Mr. Fargo. We shall be ready to leave by then."

Son of a bitch, Fargo thought. This little man really was interested in getting to Leadville. And soon.

"One hour," Fargo repeated. "I'll meet you in front of the Casa Grande."

"We shall be there, ready to venture forth," Porter said. He rose and shook Fargo's hand, then hurried away.

Odd duck, Fargo thought as he watched the dandy weave out through the patrons of the cafe. Still and all, this looked like it could be the easiest few days of work Fargo had ever had.

Skye Fargo stood and headed back for his room. He had some preparations of his own to make if they were going to crack the whips in an hour.

Damned if they weren't on time. Fargo hadn't honestly expected that. With just about any group he had ever dealt with, getting everyone together and aiming them all in one direction sometimes seemed like the hardest part of the job.

Yet when Fargo walked out of the shop across the street from the Casa Grande—which was not particularly grand, but was the best Taos had to offer—there they were.

There was no sign of a wagon, either. Porter had given in so easily on that point that Fargo had more than half-expected to see them show up driving the wagon and explaining that there simply had not been time to find mules.

Yet there they were, five people and five saddled horses, and a string of three pack mules to boot. Fargo shook his head in awe. It really did look like this was going to be the easiest money he'd ever earned.

His interest perked up to a higher pitch when he went across the street to the hitch rail where he had tied the Ovaro pinto, and led the dependable horse to the group.

"Ah, Mr. Fargo." Porter sounded delighted to see him. "May I introduce our little company." Porter motioned first to a pair of tall, distinguished-looking gentlemen so handsome they were damn near pretty.

"Elliot Croft," Porter said, and the older of the two nodded in Fargo's direction. He wore a neatly trimmed mustache and had touches of gray in his sideburns.

"Charles X. Lofton," Porter said. The second man, a few years younger than Croft but no less handsome, clicked his heels in a European gesture and bowed slightly.

"A pleasure," Fargo mumbled.

His attention, though, was behind the two men. A pair of ladies stood in capes and gloves and were carrying parasols.

"Our leading lady," Porter announced with a commanding voice. "Miss Ophelia Marie Margot."

The leading lady, chin high, swept forward to strike a pose in front of the men.

She was no spring chicken, Fargo saw. She looked to be in her forties. And being in the theater, that probably meant she wouldn't see fifty again. But damn, she was preserved as well as strawberry jam.

Miss Ophelia Marie Margot was tall and buxom, her hair a confection of blond waves and tight curls. Her lips were full and her eyes as blue as the Trailsman's. He couldn't see much of her figure, but he could imagine what it would be. And just that much was enough to warm his blood and make him wish the trip would be a long one.

She looked at him boldly but with the self-assurance of royalty. Fargo got the impression that what this woman wanted, she damned well got.

"And finally, sir," Porter went on, "our delectable ingenue, who is as talented as she is lovely, Miss Catherine Boylston Loy."

The last member of the troupe came forward to greet Fargo with a curtsy and a charmingly dimpled smile.

If Fargo's blood had been warmed by Miss Margot, it threatened to boil at the sight of Miss Loy.

She looked to be about twenty—hell, probably more like thirty—years younger than the leading lady. And her youth was not at all wasted on her.

Her hair was as light as Miss Margot's, perhaps even paler, and was done more simply. Her brown eyes were huge, wide as a river and deep enough to swim in. Her mouth and nose were rather small, the lips full and slightly pouty.

27

Where Ophelia Margot came across as bold and haughty, Catherine Loy was shy and delicate. She looked briefly at Fargo, then her eyes fell away from his. She batted her long lashes prettily and turned her face slightly so that he saw her in profile. Her nose turned up lightly at the tip, and her cheeks were rounded.

Helluva filly, Fargo thought

Her cape was buttoned to the throat, so he had no notion of what the rest of her might be like. But he had no doubts at all that he would be damned well willing to find out what lay hidden beneath the heavy wool garment. He felt sure the rest of her would not be a disappointment.

He looked briefly toward the two men. This was, after all, a group of damned good-looking adults who lived and traveled together year in and year out. It was too early for him to make any guesses about the sleeping arrangements of this crowd. And while Skye Fargo was never one to worry too much about whose toes he might be stepping on, there rarely seemed to be any purpose in asking for a knife or a bullet to come looking for one in the dark.

Neither of the actors, though, displayed any noticeable degree of possessiveness when the women were introduced.

"The Porter Players," Amon Porter announced in a booming voice. He removed his hat and with a broad, sweeping gesture pointed them out to Fargo as a group.

At their cue, the four of them bowed toward their new guide and protector.

"Troupe," Porter said, "I present to you Mr. Skye Fargo, the Trailsman." His polished tone of voice made it sound like a title of great honor instead of a simple nickname picked up over the years.

The men nodded toward him, Ophelia Margot winked at him, and Catherine Loy blushed slightly, dropping her eyes away from his once again.

"My pleasure, folks," Fargo said. "Now if you would all be good enough to climb onto those horses, we'll start heading north."

The group of players separated into individuals and headed for their horses. Fargo noted that none of the men, including Porter, offered to lend any assistance to the ladies.

Both women had sidesaddles on their mounts. Fargo helped Ophelia Margot onto her stocky bay first, then lifted Catherine Loy onto the seat of her sorrel. Miss Margot's hand lingered on his shoulder as he helped her. Miss Loy seemed to be pretending that she was being touched by a machine, her eyes avoided contact with his as she seated herself, hooked her knee onto the spoonlike projection of the saddle, and took up her reins with both hands.

"The usual way to handle these critters is with one hand on the reins, miss," Fargo said.

She frowned and cut her eyes sideways, although still without connecting with his. "I ride quite well, thank you, Mr. Fargo. One does not ride to hounds whilst slouching, sir, as seems to be the custom here. Nor does one ride lazily, with a single hand controlling the bridle and the bits."

"I'm sure you're right, miss, but there's only the one bit in that horse's mouth, and if you go to plow-rein him, he might get cranky and dump you. He won't be used to that. So if it's all the same to you, if you insist on doing things your own way, I'd suggest you ride alongside any snowdrifts you can find. The ground is likely frozen and pretty hard right now.''

Out of the corner of his eye Fargo saw both Porter and Miss Margot change the way they were holding their reins. Both of them, too, he gathered, had learned to ride in the English fashion.

Croft and Lofton looked like neither of them knew enough about horses or riding to fuck up on purpose. The two actors sat their saddles like a pair of grain sacks.

Putting up with folks who didn't know horse apples from apple sauce was just part of the job, though. Fargo went to each man and adjusted their stirrups to a proper length, then checked the cinches of every horse in the party. If any of the animals got galls on their backs, the fault would be his. That was what he was paid for.

"All right," he said finally. "I reckon we're about as ready as we're likely to get." He swung lightly into his comfortable Mexican saddle and led the way north out of the pueblo.

Porter was handling the lead line of the pack mules, he saw. And Miss Loy persisted in handling her reins with both hands. He'd given his advice. The way he saw it, it was none of his never-mind if she chose to ignore it.

It was not yet noon, and they were on their way. With any degree of luck, they would be in Leadville by noon of the fourth day out.

Ahead lay a few low, open passes, then the broad sweep of the San Luis Valley, one high pass, and finally an easy jog up the Arkansas River Valley.

Hell, even the weather didn't look to be all that bad, in spite of what the pueblo medicine men were saying.

There was a crisp bite in the air, but the temperature was probably in the low 40s or high 30s. Certainly nothing to worry about there.

And the sky was a clear and cloudless pale blue.

Helluva nice day to be setting out on the trail, actually, Fargo thought, and began to whistle a half-remembered tune under his breath. As soon as they cleared the last jacal of the village, he bumped the Ovaro into a smooth, ground-eating jog.

2

The little procession moved swiftly north. The horses and mules would have a short day of it, so Fargo moved them along at a swift, steady pace across the series of humps. They were too small for him to consider them mountains, too low to think of them as passes. Soon the Porter Players and guide dropped down onto the southern extremities of the vast San Luis Valley and rode with the massive bulk of the Sangre de Cristos looming over their right shoulders.

Fargo gave them no time for food or for conversation, stopping only once to water the horses and mules and to let the riders stretch.

Amon Porter and the ladies seemed comfortable enough, but both men were stiff-legged and sore. The two mumbled but did not protest when Fargo announced it was time to mount again.

The sky remained blue overhead, but a thin wall of gray haze began to build toward the west as the afternoon shadows lengthened. And there was a definite, sharp drop in the temperature. Fargo recalled the Indian warnings and frowned.

At least there was one kind of Indian problem he didn't have to worry about here. The wild and unpredictable Plains tribes would never think of venturing into the mountains at this season, and the mountain Utes were generally peaceful—and a long way from the San Luis. So far the trip seemed as relaxing and peaceable as Fargo had hoped.

Easy money, he muttered to himself. Funny, though, he couldn't make himself believe that, no matter how many times he insisted to himself that it was so.

He shook off his worry and ordered the party to make camp as the sun began to set behind the mountains to the west. It still would be the better part of an hour until true sundown, the late-afternoon light flooding softly past the obstruction of the peaks. With a seasoned group he likely would have pushed them harder, but he had no idea how these people would manage camp chores, and it would be pushing luck for him to ask them to learn in total darkness

To Fargo's surprise, they were reasonably competent. Croft and Lofton broke out a grimy Sibley tent that they erected for themselves and Porter, while the road manager helped the women put up a canvas wall tent.

Fargo built a fire in the lee of a stand of gnarled cottonwoods, and the men strung a picket line for the horses.

The women didn't even ask—as Fargo had half-expected—where they might find the ''necessary room.'' They just went off quietly into the brush without comment.

Easy money, Fargo told himself again. But he still didn't believe it.

Ophelia Margot took charge of the cooking. Porter had brought along thick slabs of steak wrapped in oilcloth, and Skye Fargo grinned. Maybe this was easy money, Fargo thought. This time he very nearly did believe it.

The men piled the packs and panniers between the tents. Porter unfastened several small leather cases from behind his saddle and Ophelia's before he allowed the saddles to be stored as well.

"Won't nothing be bothered," Fargo told him as he saw Porter head for the tents with the cases.

"Perhaps not, sir," Porter said, "but you fail to realize how very precious these two possessions are to us. This bag of mine is our script case. It is the very life blood of any troupe of players. It remains at my side day or night, you see."

"The other is my responsibility," Ophelia said. Her voice, Fargo noted, was surprisingly powerful and deep. "The second case contains our makeup. Freezing could separate the oils. So I sleep with the case under my blankets."

"Sounds mighty uncomfortable," Fargo said.

"All things of great value require payment in one coin or another, Mr. Fargo." The woman's expression and voice were deadpan. But damned if there wasn't something in her eyes—Fargo wasn't sure what this woman really meant. It was definitely different dealing with folks whose trade was making people believe things that weren't so, he decided. These folks were just plain harder to read than most.

"Supper is ready," Ophelia called.

They crowded close, and Ophelia handed around tin plates overflowing with fried meat and fried potatoes. She served Amon Porter first, then Fargo, then Catherine Loy. Croft and Lofton got theirs last, which

Fargo thought mildly strange. He sensed no tensions within the group, yet the two handsome men had received their suppers after Miss Loy, which was hardly normal practice.

But then Fargo had no idea what would be considered normal in a bunch of actors and actresses.

The steak was a welcome treat on the trail, and Fargo wolfed it down. He set his plate aside and left the others to their quiet conversations while he went to check on the picketed horses and mules. Then, by habit, he took a wide circle around the camp to make sure they had no unwelcome visitors in the night.

There were no more threats than he would have expected. Once he startled a young jackrabbit and soon afterward heard the flutter of an owl's wings and the high-pitched squeal of the rabbit. But other than that there was nothing.

He went back to the camp and gathered his bedroll.

"We have more than enough room in our tent for you to join us," Lofton said.

"No, thanks. I like it out where I can see and hear. Just in case."

"As you wish, of course."

Croft frowned and gave his companion a sullen look. The brief expression didn't escape the Trailsman's attention. Probably, Fargo decided, Croft didn't like to be crowded.

He carried his oilcloth-wrapped sougan and blankets into the shelter of the trees, nearer the horses than the people, and made himself a bed among last year's soggy leaves and bits of broken twigs.

Behind him he could hear a woman's voice commence a sweet song, the tone as pure as crystal. It took him a moment to realize that the words were decidedly bawdy, and the other players began to laugh.

Smiling to himself and shaking his head, Fargo set his gun belt beside his head, kicked off his boots, and crawled into his blankets. Tomorrow promised to be a long day.

His hand was on the butt of the Colt even before his eyes came open. Someone was approaching his bed, the footsteps loud on the leaves and twigs under the bare branches of the trees.

"Are you awake?" The voice was a whisper. A woman's whisper.

Fargo relaxed a little. But he didn't replace the revolver in its holster. "Come ahead."

It was very dark, and he had no way to judge how much time might have passed since he fell asleep. The stars had been obscured by clouds since he came to bed. The air that reached his face and hands was bitterly cold.

"Could you help me?" she asked. With a giggle she added, "I can't get warm."

Fargo cocked his head to one side for a moment and concentrated on listening. She was alone. There were no other creeping footsteps in the night, no sounds of tense, worried breathing. Satisfied, he shoved the Colt into the holster and reached for a match, which he thumbed aflame.

"Thank you." Catherine Loy hurried forward and dropped to her knees beside him.

Catherine? He wouldn't have been surprised to find Ophelia Margot at his side demanding that her hungers be quenched, but the shy Catherine?

She was wearing her cape. She pulled it open and let it drop from her shoulders as she crawled quickly under the sougan beside him. The match blew out, but not before he had a chance to see that she was wearing a heavy, flannel nigthtdress that covered her from throat to toenails. He still had no way to judge what her figure was like.

Catherine snuggled happily against his side with her arms wrapped around him and her pretty face nuzzling into his neck.

Whatever she was built like, she was damn sure warm.

"You still have your clothes on," she accused.

"So do you."

Catherine giggled. "Can we do something about that? It's *so* much warmer the other way."

It took Fargo only seconds to correct that problem. While he undressed, Catherine wriggled deeper under the blankets, squirming and thrashing like a cat trying to escape from a bag. But when he rejoined her, she was naked, her flesh smooth and soft to his touch. The discarded nightdress was a tangle of cloth at his feet.

Her body was warm against his. Fargo laid his hand on the flat of her belly. It was taut and slightly concave, a sure sign of youth. Her pelvic bones were sharp and prominent.

He let his hand rove higher, up to the ladder of her rib cage—she was much skinnier than he'd expected—and to the swell of her breasts. Her breasts were full, firm almost to the point of being hard. She giggled again with delight as he ran his palm across the erect, pointed juts of her nipples.

She pulled the sougan higher, covering them completely, and sighed when Fargo dipped his head to suck on her nipples and roll them between his lips.

"Oooo, I like that. Do it again, will you?"

He did, his hand drifting slowly south until he found the warm nest of curling hair. He dipped a finger into her, letting her own juices provide the lubrication he needed, then withdrew it and began to rub lightly at the tiny button of her pleasure that acted like a miniature guard at the gateway to the pleasures she could give.

Catherine began to moan, her hips pulsated as if with a mind of their own.

He was prepared to be patient with her, but there was no need for patience. Within a few minutes she shuddered and cried out as she reached a quick climax.

Her arms tightened around him and she sobbed into the hollow of his neck. "You don't know, you just don't *know* how I've been needing that."

"Don't tell me about it," he said. "Show me."

She lay flat on the hard ground under the blankets and pulled him over her, opening herself to him and using eager hands to guide him.

She gasped once when she felt the size of him, then sighed again with satisfaction as he filled her. "Mmmm," she murmured.

She raised her legs, clamping them tight around him and locking her feet together at the ankles. The movement dislodged the sougan and allowed a gust of cold air to reach them. Catherine shivered and pulled him closer, running her tongue over his throat and onto his chest.

Fargo lay socketed deep inside her. He lowered his head to suck on her breasts. It was Catherine who began to move first, her body making its own unspoken demands of him.

When he began to plunge into her, each stroke filling her, each withdrawal accompanied by a moist, sucking sound, she writhed and cried out, urging him to take her faster and deeper and harder.

He drove himself into her, feeling the hard ridge of bone over her pelvis against his belly with every downward stroke, until she was having to bite her lips to keep from screaming and until he could hold back no more.

Fargo thrust forward one last time, lunging deep inside her with a grunt as the hot fluids poured out to fill her body.

"Nice," she whispered. "So nice."

He pulled away and lay beside her with his softening cock lying on her belly.

Catherine sighed and reached down to touch him. She explored him with her fingertips, touching, feeling, pulling back his foreskin to play with the limp bulb. Then, giggling, she raised her fingers to her mouth and deliberately, loudly, sucked them clean.

"Mmmm, better than champagne, any old time." She wriggled lower under the sougan until he could feel the heat of her breath against the moisture that was cooling on his cock.

She pressed her face against him, licked his balls and then his shaft, taking long and thorough minutes before she finally pulled him inside her mouth.

Fargo was ready again long before that time.

But, hell, he was in no hurry.

Again the troupe of players surprised him. They were up before the first light of dawn, a breakfast fire crackling before Fargo first opened his eyes. He stretched and smiled as he wakened. He was alone under the protective covering of the sougan, but there was a pleasantly hollow sensation deep inside his groin that was testimony to the pleasures of the night before. He hadn't had much sleep. Neither had Catherine.

Fargo pulled his trousers on before he pushed the covers back, then stood to finish dressing. The bite of the cold was sharp against his skin. It felt good, but so did the warmth of shirt and boots and heavy, sheepskin-lined coat.

The cold was intense. In the thin, gray morning light he could see there was a solid overcast that was low and threatening. Wisps of cloud hanging down from the solid mass scudded swiftly across the low sky from west to east, although down at ground level there was as yet little wind.

Fargo raised his face to the weather and drew a deep breath of the chilly, invigorating air. It felt good at the moment, but the dire predictions of the Indians could prove correct if there was no break in the clouds. He looked toward the west and could see no change, no thinning of the cloud cover from where he stood to the shrouded peaks of the San Juans. The cloud cover was so low that he could see only the base of the distant mountains. The breathtaking view that normally could be seen from the floor of the immense valley was chopped off abruptly at a level a thousand feet or so above the floor of the San Luis.

Fargo gathered his bed and rolled it, returning it to the protection of its oilcloth, then walked to the fire. Lofton handed him a cup of stout, steaming coffee. Croft turned his face away.

Catherine, too, was ignoring him this morning. Obviously there were to be no public displays of affection, no matter what had passed between them during the night. Fargo accepted her cue and took a seat on a dead log beside Amon Porter, who was already finishing a quick breakfast.

"We'll be ready to go in ten minutes," Porter said.

"I'm impressed," Fargo admitted. "Usually I spend half my time trying to shake folks around and get them to moving."

Porter smiled. "Our trade requires that we live on the road, Mr. Fargo. Except for the lack of our wagon, this is all quite common to us." Porter left him and began putting packsaddles on the mules and riding saddles onto the horses, while the women quickly cleared away the cooking utensils and the men carried the packs and collapsed tents to the picket line. Fargo barely had time enough to finish his breakfast before Catherine whisked his plate away and stored it, still unwashed, in the last of the packs.

Damn, Fargo told himself. These folks were as efficient a crowd as he had ever seen. They might need a guide to find their way, but they damn sure didn't need a keeper.

He helped the ladies onto their sidesaddles and watched as Porter and the two men mounted, then swung onto his Ovaro.

"If you're ready, folks, I—"

He was interrupted by the snort of Catherine Loy's sorrel. The horse humped its back and gave a mighty lunge into the thin, cold air. Catherine went flying, her cape extended like a bat's wings, and landed on the rocky ground just short of a protective pad of crusty snow.

"Son of a bitch!"

Catherine lay asprawl, her hair a mess and her stockinged limbs exposed. Her skirt was in her lap.

The rest of the party broke up laughing. Fargo kept a straight face. Patiently he climbed back down from the saddle and helped the girl to her feet. She was limping slightly as he took her back to the sorrel and once again helped her up. When she was in the saddle again she looked at him for the first time that morning. "You said to put the reins in one hand?"

"Uh huh."

"Thank you."

"Yes'm." Fargo touched the brim of his stetson and returned to the Ovaro. "If you're ready now, folks." He kneed the pinto into a walk and then quickly into a lope. The horses were fresh and feisty in the cold, and he wanted to work that off them.

Before noon the swiftly moving party was approaching the old town of San Luis with its jacales and low, adobe-walled permanent buildings. The town had been there longer than any living man could remember, which was a great rarity in this isolated country.

Fargo drew the pinto to a halt and waited for Porter to catch up with him. He pointed to the bell tower of the ancient church, which was the center of the community.

"We can noon there," he said. "Quicker and easier than stopping to build a fire."

"Nonsense," Porter told him. "Pass it by, Mr. Fargo."

"But—"

"Please, sir," Porter interrupted. "Detour around if you can, in fact."

"Why? It'll be quicker to eat there."

"You do not understand, Mr. Fargo. I assume you have little experience with troupes of players such as ours, but trust me on this. We shall proceed much more quickly if we ride wide of the town than if we stop for what you believe would be a fast meal."

Fargo was about to object as Porter smiled at him with benign patience and continued, "You have no idea, sir, of the fame of these players or the excitement their presence would cause in such a town."

Fargo scratched his chin. He hadn't had time to shave that morning, and the beginning stubble was mildly annoying. "Reckon I don't know what you mean," he admitted.

"Believe me, Mr. Fargo, if we were to appear in that village, we would quickly be surrounded by admirers and supplicants. Small children would beseige us. The town fathers would gather to plead for us to stay and to perform for them. Loutish young men would pester the ladies, and pretty señoritas would bat their eyes at the gentlemen. Aside from the jealousies this would cause, possibly leading to unpleasantnesses, sir, it would be very difficult for us to extricate ourselves from the burg without causing ill will. Believe me when I tell you that our presence in that village would delay us unnecessarily."

"I really don't think—"

"Please." Porter was still smiling, but there was a firmness in his voice that said his mind was made up regardless of what arguments Fargo might put forward.

The Trailsman shrugged. "It don't make that much difference to me."

"Thank you."

Fargo reined the Ovaro in a wide, sweeping arc that would carry them around San Luis to the east.

It was damned odd, though, he considered as he rode. Any halfway normal group of dudes would have been delighted at the chance to sit at a table and eat a meal they hadn't cooked themselves.

Folks not accustomed to the Big Empty that lay between the infrequent towns of this huge and sprawling raw land were invariably overjoyed at the sight of a building, much less by an opportunity to stop inside one.

Hell, the usual problem was to pry them out of each stopover.

But not this crowd. No trouble getting them moving in the morning. Now this refusal to stop for a meal in comfortable surroundings. Fargo didn't understand it.

On the other hand, they were damn sure an easy bunch to guide. He'd never come across a group that was so simple to lead. Just a point a direction and turn them loose.

He should have been tickled by that. Instead he was becoming suspicious.

They rode on, though, as Porter wanted, and soon left San Luis behind.

They nooned briefly, taking time only to let the horses and mules blow for a few minutes with their cinches loose and to quickly eat cold bacon left over from the breakfast fire. No one suggested they build a fire, although midday was no warmer than the morning had been.

44

Nagged by his inner instinct, Fargo found himself concentrating on their back trail as they continued on. He always paid attention to everything he could see or sense from one horizon to the other, but now he was paying particular attention to the south, back toward Taos, the way they'd come.

Off to the west Fargo could see a moving wall of grayish, dirty white that now completely obscured the San Juan Mountains from View.

"Snow," he said, pointing.

Porter nodded and turned up the collar of his coat. Behind him the others did the same.

"If you're worried," Fargo said, "we can still turn back to San Luis and hole up there. Wait it out."

"Not at all," Porter said. "We have no fear of the weather, and I trust you shall not lose direction."

"No," Fargo said, "I reckon I know where we're going. Just wanted to give you the chance."

"Press on, sir. We must be in Leadville as quickly as possible."

"Whatever you say."

The leading edge of the snowfall reached them by midafternoon. The first flakes were soft and light and dry, fluttering down on light currents of breeze.

Quickly the breeze turned to wind, and the snowflakes became smaller and harder. The wind drove them into Fargo's left ear and numbed the side of his face. He pulled an oversized bandanna from his pocket and tied it over his head, covering his ears. He then rummaged in his saddlebags for a pair of heavy, buffalo-hide gauntlets with the dense, dark wool of the hair turned inside. The gauntlets were large, unwieldy mittens with only a thumb covering protruding from the side of the crude pouch. They were warmer than any glove. The right mitten had been made very large, much larger than necessary, so that if the need should arise, a flick of his wrist would send it flying, freeing his right hand so he could manipulate a gun.

The Porter Players, he noted, were making similar arrangements as they rode, the ladies finding scarves, the men kerchiefs, to cover their throats and ears. Their gloves, though, were thin, attractive affairs more suitable for strolling in polite company than for serious warmth. Still, if they insisted on going on, they would have to make do with what they had. Fargo's job was to guide them, not nurse them. He kept the stout Ovaro's nose pointed north and tucked his chin inside the shelter of his upturned coat collar.

It was getting colder now, and there was a real bite in the wind. The small, hard spicules of snow drove sideways in front of them, lashed by the wind. Within minutes small drifts began to build in the lee of every rock, downwind from every ripple in the flat surface of the land.

If this kept up, Fargo thought, they could be in for a serious blow.

He held the pinto back, again allowing Porter to gain on him.

"Looks like we're in for one hell of a storm," Fargo said, having to raise his voice to make himself heard. "We could still go back if you want."

Porter shook his head, his jaw clamped tight and his lips thin in stubborn refusal. "We go on."

"All right."

The horses had instinctively dropped back into a stolid, steady walk, plodding forward with their muzzles turned slightly away from the crosswind. Fargo let them take the pace that they seemed to find comfortable, not pushing them or asking more of them than they willingly gave. Those old Indians sure knew what they were talking about Fargo said to himself. And maybe the horses sensed something too. If the beasts felt a need to conserve themselves, Fargo wasn't going to deny them that need.

The party plodded forward into the cold, white rush of the driven snow, their visibility reduced to little more than the horses before and behind them, their only guide the Trailsman's sense of blind direction—north, always north.

It was impossible to see how much daylight remained, and Fargo didn't own a watch. He rode on until he thought it must be nearing sundown. All he could see, all he had seen for some time except for the white, crusted figures coming along behind him, was a shifting, blowing sweep of snow. Driven through the air, skittering madly across the frozen ground—everywhere it was the same—a fluid mass of quickly moving white.

He turned in his saddle and looked behind. Amon Porter and his horse were a ghostly shape barely visible through the translucent curtain of the blowing snow. There was the similarly ghostly shape of a led mule behind him. And behind that mule a vague, dim shape that Fargo knew was the next mule in line. If he hadn't already known what was following, though, he wouldn't have been able to tell what that half-seen form represented. There was no sign at all of the ladies and men who trailed behind Porter's mules. He had to take it on blind faith that they were all still in line, that none of them had been so foolish as to let themselves become separated from the rest of the party.

As he had several times before, Fargo made sure by motioning Porter to a halt. Then he turned the rugged, snow-plastered Ovaro and rode back along the short row. The pinto was usually the most handsome of animals, its distinctive coloration truly beautiful with jet, gleaming black on its head and forequarters back to the withers, then a band of purest white to the crupper, and again the gleaming black on its hindquarters. Now, though, the entire left side of the animal was as white as if it had been painted, from muzzle to tail. Only on its right side, protected from the wind-driven snow by the bulk of its own body, was the pinto's coat visible.

Fargo rode back along the hunched and shivering line of people, past Porter and the mules, past Ophelia Margot and Catherine Loy, past Lofton, and to Croft at the end of the little procession.

They were all there. Each of them looked perfectly miserable. None had the will left to turn their faces into the force of the snow to look at him as he rode by checking on them.

Fargo, satisfied that they were all still there, turned the Ovaro north again and moved slowly up until he was beside Porter.

"Come ahead." He had to shout to make himself heard. The wind whipped the words from his mouth almost before he could speak them. If he'd been three feet away from Porter on the downwind side of the man's horse, Fargo doubted that Porter would have been able to hear him.

Like the others, Porter didn't turn his face to look at

Fargo. The man had something, an extra shirt possibly, muffled around his neck and the lower part of his face so that only his eyes showed above the cloth. His hat was pulled low. His eyebrows and the entire left side of his wrapped face was caked with snow.

Fargo waited until Porter silently nodded in acknowledgment, then led the way forward.

The Ovaro plodded on, steady and dependable. Fargo knew the horse would carry him straight through to Leadville if that was what was demanded of it. The pinto would continue straight on to the end of the trek or until it died of exhaustion, whichever came first. The horse's willingness, its largeness of heart, made it the Trailsman's responsibility to see that he didn't push the horse beyond the limits of bone and muscle.

He rode on, searching with his other senses, since eyesight couldn't tell him anything, until he felt a slight lessening of the push of wind against his left side.

The roar and whistle of the wind remained as high as before, but he was sure he could feel less power in it. They must have been downwind from some unseen obstruction that was disrupting the passage of the storm. Whatever that obstruction was, it couldn't be far away or he wouldn't have been able to notice the difference in the wind.

He stopped and rode back again the length of the group, warning each one with sign language. Then he motioned Porter to follow and turned the Ovaro so that the pinto was forcing his way head down and blinking into the teeth of the storm.

The horse plodded hock-deep in swirling snow, then stopped. Fargo tried to knee the Ovaro forward, but it braced itself and nervously refused, tossing its head in anger at being given an instruction it couldn't follow.

Fargo tried to peer forward into the wind, but he could see nothing but white. He wiped the snow from his face and looked again.

There was something dark ahead. He had thought that the light was failing; instead there was something there, some insubstantial and only partially seen shape.

And he was aware now that there was a definite reduction in the force of the gale. He was so numbed by cold that he hadn't been sure of that, but it was so.

Slowly, his numbed legs protesting, he dismounted and felt his way forward, careful to keep his hold on the Ovaro's reins. The horse had stopped, its chest pressed against a low wattle fence.

Beyond the fence there was a tall, rounded mass. A building?

Fargo ground-reined the pinto and crawled awkwardly over the fence. He advanced half a dozen steps. In the lee of the dark shape that loomed over him, there was practically no wind at all. The sudden change from cold, blowing fury to this still air was almost warm, although only in comparison.

At first he thought they had found a huge sod structure. Then he felt the pile and realized that they had lucked instead onto someone's haystack.

The few inhabitants of the San Luis, mostly Mexican families who had been on this land for generations before the first white explorers reached the broad valley, raised gardens and meats for their own consumption, and mostly beans as their cash crops. The beans stored well and were light to transport south toward Taos and Santa Fe.

Here it seemed that some enterprising farmer had harvested his crop and piled the stems as a crude form of hay for winter feed. The fence would have been built around the stack to keep the cattle from helping themselves. An undercut all around the circumference of the stack showed that deer were not kept out by the wattle fencing. The area where the deer had been eating, however, created an overhang that would make a perfect place for the placement of beds tonight. The hay itself would serve the needs of the horses. Poor as beans-stem hay was, it was much better than anything they would be able to forage for themselves on a night like this.

Fargo went back to the waiting troupe and motioned for them to dismount. One at a time, beginning with Porter, the people rode to the fence and got off their mounts. Fargo took the animals and tied them in the relative protection of the downwind side of the haystack, even though that meant making them face the wind through the night. He dropped saddles and packs on the other side of the fence and helped the people over and into the protection formed by the bulk of the haystack.

Lofton fumbled with the packs, trying to get to one of the tents with numbed fingers encased in the thinnest of gloves.

"No." Fargo had to lean down and shout into the man's ear before he responded. "No tent tonight. Damn thing'd blow clear to Kansas if you tried to put it up."

Lofton hesitated for a moment, then nodded.

"Get the food bags," Fargo told him. "No fire tonight either, but we'll be able to eat."

Croft and Porter got the party's bedding from the packs. Their beds were so many blankets bundled together, suitable for use inside a wagon or tent but not what Fargo would have chosen for the kind of night they would have to spend. Still, poor bedding was better than none. They would have to make do. He got his own heavy bedroll and carried it to the downwind side of the tall stack.

A snowdrift was forming between the stack and the fence, but the eddying wind left a clear space directly at the base of the stack. It was here that Fargo laid his bedroll, his head sheltered by the overhang caused by the marauding deer and his feet toward the drift.

"Lay yours out the same," he said. "There isn't room enough for everybody to get underneath, so we'll all lie down side by side. No way to have a fire tonight, but by morning, if we're lucky, the snow will've drifted high enough to block the backflow from over the top of the stack. So maybe we can have a fire and a hot meal for breakfast. Miss Margot, I take it you're in charge of the food, so you can figure out what we have for supper. Something that doesn't need cooking."

The handsome woman looked utterly miserable. He could see only her eyes above a multicolored wrap of many thin scarves that had been intended for decoration rather than warmth. Like the others, she was plastered an inch or more thick with snow on her left side and all across the front of her heavy skirt. Both women had been more exposed to the storm than the men, because the sidesaddles they rode placed both their legs on the left side of their mounts.

"I don't *have* anything," she wailed. "Nothing that can be eaten without cooking."

"No bully beef or jerky or hardtack?" Fargo asked.

She shook her head. "Flour and salt and lard. Raw beef and raw bacon. Uncooked beans, rice, coffee, tea. . . ." She shook her head again.

Fargo grinned. "Well, hell, folks, raw meat's not so bad, if you're hungry."

Catherine turned her head away. Croft made a face and shuddered.

"Got to wait until the wind dies then, or that drift builds high enough to give some help," Fargo said.

Fargo opened the food pack and helped himself to a slab of steak. The meat was nearly frozen, so he tucked it inside his shirt to warm up while he supervised the laying out of the beds.

"Best thing," he said, "will be to double up tonight. Warmer that way, and I expect everybody was planning to sleep with boots on anyhow."

Croft and Lofton automatically laid their beds out together, and the women paired off, leaving Fargo to share his bed with Amon Porter. There were two pairings Fargo might have preferred, but this hardly seemed the time to worry about that.

Fargo helped himself to armloads of the bean-stem hay, taken from the sides of the stack and not over the beds, and gave ample helpings to the tied animals. He had to make several trips from the stack to the fence before he was satisfied that the stock would be all right. Even in those few minutes he could tell that the size of the drift behind the stack was growing. They likely would be able to have a fire by morning, he judged.

By the time he was done feeding and setting up the camp, his body heat had thawed the beef sufficiently that he could chew it with comfort. He used his knife in the old, mountain-man fashion, biting first into the raw meat, then using the sharp blade to saw off the tough meat at his lips.

A little blood had trickled to his chin, and Fargo winked at Ophelia Margot as he wiped it away with the sleeve of his coat.

He was teasing the woman, expecting her to be shocked. Instead she surprised him by laughing. Fargo grinned and held the chunk of raw, dark meat out to her. She declined it but didn't seem at all offended by the sight.

Catherine Loy reached forward to touch his sleeve. Again he was surprised. "I'll try some," she said.

"All right." He used the knife to shave off several small bites of the meat. Catherine popped one into her mouth and chewed uncertainly for a moment. Then a look of amazement came over her pretty features.

"Why, that isn't bad at all."

" 'Course not," he said. "And tenderer than cooked. More?"

She nodded, and Fargo shared his meal with her. The others looked on dourly.

"Don't worry," Fargo said. "It'll be better in the morning."

"Do you think the storm will break?" Porter asked. The man sounded curious but, oddly, not hopeful that it would.

Fargo shrugged. "Time to time, they can blow like this for days on end. No way to tell yet. What I meant was that either way we can likely have us a fire in the morning."

Porter nodded.

"Then I certainly hope we can delay long enough for hot beverages," Ophelia Margot said.

"Tea for me, please," Catherine added.

The two male players were huddled together whispering something, Fargo saw. They were curiously detached from the group.

Fargo decided that he really didn't understand these theatrical folks at all. He yawned and stretched. "You can set up all you like, but me, I'm turning in now." He crawled onto the wide bed he would share with Porter, removed his coat and gun belt, then slipped under the warm, welcome bulk of the sougan. Porter's bedding comprised the bottom of their shared bed, Fargo's much superior bedroll the top.

As Fargo expected, there was no round of sweet singing before the Porter Players came to bed.

And, unfortunately, there was no nocturnal visitation from Catherine either.

3

Amon Porter snored. But he didn't smell bad. So, all in all, things could have been worse. Still, Fargo was glad when the morning came. He was up at the first hint of light, which amounted to a lessening of the darkness rather than any true dawn. The wind and the snow were still blowing, if with a bit less fury than the night before.

As soon as Fargo stirred, Porter came awake too and quickly shook the others awake.

Fargo pulled on his coat and mittens, then had to take the mittens off again to tie the bandanna over his ears. He stood and looked into the sky. It was hard to tell for sure, but he thought there was little snow falling now. Most of what was blowing past was probably in the form of a ground blizzard, the high wind picking up previously fallen snow and carrying it into the deepening drifts. Fargo inhaled deeply and decided that the temperature was not too bad either, above zero anyway. He could tell because the hairs inside his nostrils remained unfrozen.

The drift between the haystack and the fence was high enough that Fargo couldn't see the horses and mules. He gathered an armload of hay from the side of the stack and floundered with it through the edge of the drift to assure himself that the animals were still there and waiting to be fed.

He distributed the first armload of fodder to them and gathered a return load of firewood from the fence. The wattle structure was made from short pieces of dry, twisted wood set upright in the ground and attached to a single horizontal stringer. It was a long way to the nearest timber on this flat, barren stretch of valley floor, so the farmer who had built the fence had made do with the brushy materials he could find near at hand. Fargo didn't intend to destroy the man's fence, but he had to use some of it. He yanked loose every other upright piece, leaving enough behind to keep cattle out.

He carried the wood back to the lee of the stack and dropped it there for someone else to make into a fire, then went on with the chore of feeding the animals. By his third trip the needs of the beasts, had been met, and Ophelia Margot was bending over a flickering blaze on his return. One pot of melted snow was already heating, and she heaped more snow into a second pot. Catherine was hacking chunks of raw bacon from a frozen slab and dropping the ragged results of her labors into a skillet.

"Is everything all right, Mr. Fargo?" Porter asked.

"Sure. None of the horses or mules took off during the night, if that's what you mean."

"You saw nothing?" Porter asked.

Fargo grunted. "I saw what you'd expect. Lots of white, any direction you want to look. That's about it."

"Nothing else?"

Fargo planted his hands on his hips and stood facing

Porter. "Just what is it you expected me to see out there in the middle of a damn ground blizzard?" he demanded.

"Nothing," Porter said quickly.

"Oh, tell him, Amon. For God's sake, admit it. We are, after all, dependent on Mr. Fargo," Lofton said. The man received a hard look from Croft and one of dismay from Porter, but by then the damage had been done.

"I think maybe one of you better tell me," Fargo said in a low, cutting voice. "Right now."

Porter swallowed and looked away.

"If you won't tell him, Amon, I must," Lofton said. "We heard rumors, Mr. Fargo, in Santa Fe," he said. "There is a competitor of ours, a troupe managed by a man named Wickse. Not a gentleman, mind you—Mr. Wickse is a rough customer, as the saying goes. He believes that he can secure a contract for his players with the same gentleman we plan to audition for in Leadville. He is determined—Wickse, that is—to stop us from reaching Leadville in time for that audition. He believes that if we don't receive the contract, he will. And he stands to make a great deal of money from it. We haven't been totally forthright with you, Mr. Fargo. We've been given to believe that this competing troupe may have hired a man or possibly a body of men to stop us from reaching our destination."

Porter nodded unhappily and added, "That is why I didn't want to stop in that village yesterday. Aside from the time that would be expended, I didn't want anyone to know we had passed through there on our way north."

"Didn't want anybody to know—why, you told half

of damn Taos where you was going. Why should it make any difference if they know you're on your way to Leadville now?''

Porter smiled. ''Because Mr. Wickse has reason to believe that our prospective backer is to audition us, not in Leadville but in the Comstock country. We deliberately talked openly about going to Leadville in the hope that Wickse would believe we were laying a false trail, and follow us instead westward. So you see, sir, if he has no confirmation that we are indeed traveling north, he will believe we were laying that false trail and immediately hurry west to Nevada. Which is precisely what we want him to do.''

''Because,'' Croft said, ''we really are going to Leadville.''

''That's where the audition will take place,'' Lofton concluded.

Fargo shook his head. ''Am I supposed to understand all that shit?''

Porter laughed. ''Not really, sir. You merely need to guide us to Leadville as agreed.''

''But there could be somebody after you?'' Fargo said.

''Uh, yes.''

''How bad and how permanent are they supposed to stop you?'' Fargo asked.

''That, sir, we do not know. Obviously we were not a party to the transaction. We only heard of it through admirers of our work,'' Porter said.

This put a little different light on the job, and it explained the outfit's willingness to pay well and move damned fast, Fargo thought. It also explained some of the uneasiness he'd been feeling lately, about things like passing by San Luis and moving along in the face of a storm like this one. He shook his head.

He had half a mind to get on the pinto and ride south, down where it was warmer and there weren't any high passes to cross. Hell, he already had their money in his pocket. No one could fault him for leaving them after they'd lied to him.

No one, he conceded, except himself. No, dammit, he'd taken their money. Even if they hadn't told him everything they should have, the job was his until it was done. It wasn't danger that bothered him, it was being lied to.

But at least they'd come clean about it now. They could've kept on lying to him, and he wouldn't have known any different for some time. Why, hell, it was sure unlikely that there'd be any hired crowd of plug-uglies or even gunslingers who'd be following them in this kind of storm. Why, the weather could be one of the better favors the Porter Players ever received. A hand hired on to go out and chase a few pilgrims wasn't likely to be industrious enough to stick with the job in this kind of weather, Fargo figured, but he'd still be on guard.

"Breakfast," Ophelia Margot called, her tone of voice quite ordinary and pleasant. Either she hadn't been paying attention to the conversation or was unaffected by it.

Fargo decided that, either way, the woman's response might just be the best way to leave it for now. It probably wasn't worth worrying about. He accepted a plate of greasy but hot bacon chunks and a cup of quickly cooling coffee and went off by himself to hunker down out of the wind and eat.

The wind slacked off by late morning, and once it was gone, the temperatures, cold as they were, seemed almost balmy.

They were making good time in spite of the conditions. No land was completely flat, at least none Skye Fargo had ever seen, and the broad, flat basin of the valley was no exception. Wherever there was a scant rise above the surface of the valley floor, the wind had scoured the snow almost clear, while on either side there might be drifts as tall as a man on horseback. It was there that Fargo led them, picking his way in a snaking route between the drifted snow so that the going was easy on the horses.

Now that he knew there was the possibility that someone might be following, he was also conscious of the tracks they would leave behind. By keeping out of the drifts, they left little mark on the frozen soil beneath the horses hooves. Anyone following would have a tough time of it.

He deliberately trended westward during much of the morning's travel, just in case there was someone back there who could read sign when there was little to find.

In order to reach Poncha Pass and cross from the San Luis into the Arkansas Valley, they would eventually have to angle westward to the northwest tip of the San Luis, toward the southern foot of Poncha. By making that westward move now, he could confuse the issue for anyone following along behind. By turning now, he could make it look like they were headed for the forbidding Wolf Creek Pass across the Rio Grande headwaters and up into the San Juans. From here that was the logical route to follow if a party intended to move into southern Utah and across to the Comstock country.

Fargo didn't bother to explain his plan. He'd been pissed enough with Porter and company to refrain from speaking to any of them since the morning move-out order.

The wind slackened even more, and so did the ground blizzard. Soon they were moving under threatening but mostly inactive clouds. The sky was still completely overcast, but very little snow was falling in the form of large, soft, dry flakes.

It became comfortable enough that Fargo was able to untie the annoying bandanna and put it away. He pulled the buffalo gauntlets off and returned them to his saddlebags.

All of them, he saw, were riding more comfortably, sitting upright in their saddles. They even began to smile and talk among themselves some. Lofton laughed out loud at something Croft said. Porter turned around and said something to the women, who both broke into large smiles.

Fargo damn near laughed himself. He sure as hell was punishing them all by not chatting with them this morning. They were all kind of upset about it, he muttered to himself.

He stood in his stirrups and scanned the white, wintery horizon behind them.

Visibility was still poor; the light was lousy and a thin veil of snow softened his view of distant objects as if he were trying to see through an oiled-paper window covering. But he could see a hell of a lot better now than before. As far as he could see, there was nothing but the long, white drifts and the occasional matching lines of darker ground showing through on the higher places. Even those would soon be covered over if the wind held off and the snow continued to fall.

There was no threat anywhere within sight, Fargo noted. Nothing moved, not even the hawks and rabbits that inhabited this empty stretch—even they seemed to be still holed up.

Fargo turned and craned his head up and to the west, sniffing the air as if it would tell him whether the storm was over . . . or if it was only in a lull. The absence of game and small creatures made him suspect that the Indians' warnings had not yet been fulfilled, that there was more of this storm yet to come.

There was nothing to see in any direction, nothing but gray cloud above and white planes of fresh snow below. Their few horses and mules marked the only movement as far as Fargo could see.

The Trailsman faced forward and bumped the pinto into a lope. He had an idea that they might want to hole themselves up early tonight if they found a suitable shelter in time. It was just a hunch, but he was not about to ignore it.

"Let me ask you this one more time," Fargo said as he brought the group to a halt for the noon break. "Do you have any idea of what the intentions are of the folks that're supposed to be following you?"

Porter shook his head. "I already told you."

"All right, then," Fargo interrupted. "No fire today."

Porter gave him a questioning look.

"There's somebody behind us," Fargo told him. "Has been for a couple hours now."

Porter and both male members of the troupe stood in

their stirrups and peered back the way they had just come.

"I don't see anything," Croft said sullenly.

"Me neither," his partner affirmed.

"They're back there," Fargo assured them. "Seven, maybe eight riders, pushing hard. I've caught them silhouetted a couple times, and one or two of them smokes, or breathes damned hard. They're back there, all right, and they're gaining on us. I thought you ought to know."

Porter swallowed and looked nervously over his shoulder toward where Skye Fargo had said there were men following. "Perhaps"—he swallowed and tried again—"perhaps we should press on, not stop for lunch today."

Fargo dismounted and loosened the cinch on the pinto. "Your business if you want to skip eating, of course, but these horses need some rest."

"But if we stop to eat and those men do not. . . ."

Fargo grinned at him. "If they're dumb enough to do that, mister, count yourself lucky. This isn't a flat track where you run a horse race. This here is the kind of situation where staying power is more important than speed. It's the rested horse that has the staying power, not the fast one."

"But—"

"For God's sake, Amon, shut up and do what Mr. Fargo tells you. That's what we hired him for," Ophelia Margot snapped.

Porter sighed. "You are right, of course, my dear. Here, let me help you down."

The group dismounted, and Porter helped both women from their horses.

"Don't forget to loose your cinches," Fargo advised. "Give the horses a chance to blow and to pick at some grass if they can find any."

The men looked worriedly toward the back trail, but they followed the Trailsman's instructions.

"Do you think we can reach Leadville on schedule?" Porter asked.

Fargo shrugged. "It depends, doesn't it?"

"On what?" the little man queried.

By way of an answer, Fargo looked toward the west. The sky remained totally overcast from the low horizon to the west across the full sweep of sky to the east. Furthermore, in the west there was a darker and somewhat ominous gray quality to the low, scudding cloud.

"More snow?" Porter asked.

Again Fargo shrugged. "Could be. For that matter, could be a blessing if there is. Way things are now, we're easy enough to follow. Another snow fall and we can do a little dodging if there's wind enough to sweep our tracks. Otherwise, if they got tracks to follow, all we can do is run like hell and hope their horses are too tired to close the gap."

Lofton shivered and licked his lips, then snuffled and turned his head away.

"Or fight," Fargo said. "We haven't discussed that."

Croft turned away too, jamming his hands deep into the pockets of his coat.

Fargo said, "Well, so much for fighting."

Porter took his elbow. "Mr. Fargo, please you must understand that we are artistes, not fighters."

"Yeah."

The women had been engaged in the practical task of

putting together a cold meal while the men fretted over the things that might or might not transpire during the rest of the day. Catherine Loy passed around cold johnnycake while Ophelia Margot probed in the mule packs for anything else that might be edible without cooking. At least Miss Margot had had the foresight this morning to cook more than was needed for breakfast, Fargo noted. The women in the party seemed to be all right, although he had certain reservations about their choice of male companions.

It took the group only a matter of minutes to consume the leftover johnnycakes, but Fargo kept them there for another half-hour while the horses rested. By the time he had them mount again, the wind was picking up and visibility to the west had been reduced to less than half a mile.

Fargo motioned for them to wait while he turned the Ovaro along their back trail. He rode back to the top of the now almost imperceptible rise and stood in his stirrups to look for the pursuers.

As far as he could see to the rear, there was nothing but rolling fields of unbroken white. Nothing moved; no smoke rose.

Fargo grunted softly to himself, and the pinto's ears flicked. He leaned forward and stroked the horse's neck. "Canny sons of bitches," he muttered. "They know not to push too hard. Pity." He turned the pinto and went back to the head of his little group, rode past them, and motioned for them to follow. But this time he picked the pace up somewhat.

Wind, quickly followed by driven snow, began to swirl around them.

Pleased with the uncomfortable development, Fargo

paused at the top of a rise to assure himself that there was no visibility between their party and the pursuers. Nothing could be seen in any direction now except the blowing snow. Visibility was a hundred yards or less.

With a grunt of satisfaction, Fargo led the group down into a protected hollow and up onto the next rise. Midway up the side of the slight slope, where the wind was scouring the frozen earth, he reined the pinto toward the west and led the party in a new direction. With any kind of luck the wind would eliminate any sign of their passage. The pursuers might be thrown off.

Croft left his place in line and rode up beside Fargo. "Aren't we going the wrong way?"

Fargo gave the man a cold look. "You want to lead?"

The actor looked frightened. He shook his head quickly. "I just thought—"

"Best if you don't think," Fargo advised.

Croft nodded unhappy agreement and dropped back into place behind the pack mules led by Porter. Fargo shook his head.

They followed the westward course for the better part of an hour, then turned north again. The snow and wind continued. As far as Fargo could tell, the temperature hadn't changed three degrees since dawn. Now it began to drop as the bite of the wind intensified. The falling flakes changed too, becoming smaller and harder, and stinging harder, as the cold deepened. Fargo reached for his bandanna and gauntlets.

It was no longer possible to follow patches of bare earth. So much snow had fallen already that the ground was completely blanketed in white. The horses had to walk through as little as four or five inches in some spots, then plunge chest-deep through the drifts between those areas of lesser depth. Fargo rode at a slower pace now, closely gauging the reactions of the stout Ovaro, feeling with knee and hand and closely attuned senses as the sturdy horse began to tire.

The pinto was doing the hardest work for the bunch, having to break trail for the others to follow when they breasted a drift. But the pinto was also the strongest horse in the group. If it was beginning to tire, the others must be too.

They reached a low, snaking line of flat, unbroken snow that was covered to a depth of three feet or more. It continued north and south as far as Fargo could see, and no grass or yucca heads protruded above the surface.

That had to be the wagon road, Fargo was sure. He paused for a moment, trying to estimate how far they had come, exactly where they should be.

"North," he muttered to himself. "It should be north a couple miles." He sent the pinto across the road and onto a hillside beyond it.

On the other side of the hill there was less snow to fight, but the force of the biting wind was stronger. The wind was the lesser of their problems now, the condition of the horses most important.

He turned and raised his voice so Porter could hear. "A few more miles to shelter."

The old man smiled and turned to pass the word along.

As if it had sensed the meaning of its master's words, the pinto picked up the pace and forged ahead through the snow, ignoring the blasts of icy wind and snow that crusted its left eye almost closed.

After three miles had been traveled, Fargo began to

wonder if he'd judged wrongly and they had already passed the point he wanted.

No. There it was to the left. A dark bulk loomed behind the curtain of swirling white.

"Thank God," he heard Porter say at a moment when the wind slacked.

They rode closer. The force of the wind was broken, and behind the huge obstruction the snow came down soft and cold.

Towering above them, blocking the wind and creating a small, sheltered space in its lee, was a block of granite as large as the finest building in Kansas City—possibly larger. It rose from the earth like a gigantic thumb and was surrounded by smaller outriders no larger than a trapper's cabin. As far as Fargo could recall, this monolith was the only shelter available for miles in any direction. The nearest timber was probably another eight miles to the west. The foot of Poncha Pass was twice that to the north.

"There's a boulder a few feet off the base of the rock," Fargo said. "Build the fire there, against the boulder. It'll act as a reflector and throw the heat on us if we sit between it and the big rock. You can tuck the packs and gear under there"—he pointed—"and let the horses loose. They won't go anywhere tonight. Grain them first. They've earned it."

He pulled his saddle and put it under a slight overhang at the base of the monolith, then carefully rubbed down the pinto's back and legs before he gave the horse a gallon of the grain Porter had packed along. He cursed some when he saw the grain sacks. The man might know a great deal about the theater and acting, but he'd brought about half the amount of grain Fargo would consider normal for this trip. And in winter-storm conditions, the animals would need more grain than usual to replace lost body heat. If they hadn't been in such a damn hurry to leave Taos, Fargo would have checked their provisions which, Skye Fargo told himself bitterly, was only an excuse. The fact was, it was his responsibility. Dammit, he swore silently.

There was no wood for a fire, so they made do with dried yucca stalks, twists of grass, and a few frozen clumps of manure they were able to find by kicking through the snow cover.

Fargo was glad to see that there was grass beneath the snow. The horses and mules easily pawed down to it.

Dinner was over quickly—a fast and simple meal—and with no wood to maintain a good fire, there was no reason for Fargo to remain in the area between the boulder and the huge parent rock where the players were now laying out their bedding.

Besides, if the pursuers should happen to know about this shelter and head for it, Fargo wanted to be in a better position for defense. He carried his bedroll away from the rest of the party and laid it out on the downwind side of one of the smaller boulders near the base of the monolith.

Overhead and to either side of the huge jut of rock, the wind continued to howl. Driven snow slashed past on both sides, but overhead it eddied and then drifted quietly down.

Fargo removed his boots and coat, folded the coat for a pillow, and tucked his gun belt into it so that he could reach the weapon if need be. His Sharps carbine he laid under his blankets.

They had stopped early. It was not yet quite dark when Fargo saw a figure materialize from behind the curtain of falling snow.

He reached for the Colt, then realized that the figure was coming from the area where the Porter Players were bedded.

The person wore a white-dusted cape and was carrying two cups of steaming coffee.

Fargo grinned and held the sougan open for her to join him.

He received a mild but not unpleasant shock when the woman joined him and he realized who she was. He'd been expecting Catherine, and instead it was Ophelia Margot who had brought his coffee. And judging from the way she boldly joined him beneath the protection of the sougan, her intent was to bring more than just coffee.

"Thanks," Fargo said, accepting the coffee. He took a swallow of the beverage. In the brief time it had taken to pour it steaming from the pot and carry it to him, the coffee had already cooled. "Next time warm the cup first," the Trailsman suggested.

Ophelia Margot raised one eyebrow and gave him a haughty look of disapproval—or of disbelief.

Skye Fargo grinned at her. If this woman, accustomed to being fawned and fussed over, expected him to join the lineup of her admirers, she might be in for some surprises.

Ophelia looked disapproving for only a moment. Then she laughed and swept her cape from her shoulders, covering herself with the sougan, which she drew up to her chin. She held her own cup in both hands and looked wide-eyed over the rim at him while she sipped from it.

Her china-blue eyes locked into his lake-blue ones. There was a smoldering flirtatiousness in the look she gave him.

"Take your clothes off," Fargo said bluntly.

Ophelia gasped with shock, then quickly covered it with a peal of hearty laughter. She reached over to touch his wrist. "My dear, *dear*, impetuous *man*," she said.

"Im-pet-u-ous," Fargo said slowly, mouthing each syllable. "Fine word, that is, and here I thought I was just horny." He grinned at her again. "Thought you were too, for that matter. But, I've been wrong before."

He drank down the remainder of the lukewarm coffee and handed the empty cup back to her, then lay down under his side of the sougan, rolled onto his side with his back to the woman, and pulled the cover over his head. He could hear nothing but the wind droning overhead, but he could feel Ophelia stiffen at his side. In disbelief, he guessed, and dismay.

For several seconds Fargo could feel Ophelia trembling at his side.

Then, instead of storming away as he half-expected, she once again laughed. She moved a few inches away—probably setting the cups aside, he figured—then burrowed under the covers at his side. He could feel her breath, warm against the back of his neck.

"I've wanted you," she said in a low, throaty tone of voice, "since the first time I saw you." Her hand crept across his body to caress his chest and belly, then up again to slide over the firm swell of his biceps and onto his shoulders. "You are quite a man, Mr. Fargo. *Quite* a man."

He reached behind him and felt clothing covering the round fullness of her hip. "You're still dressed," he accused.

Ophelia chuckled and withdrew. He could feel her moving and wiggling as she unbuttoned her dress and wriggled out of it. This time, when he touched her, he found only warm flesh beneath his fingers.

"Better," he said.

He rolled over to face her. Their lips and eyes were only inches apart. Both were open. Both were welcoming.

Fargo kissed her, and Ophelia's eyes closed, her tongue darting, probing between his lips.

He cupped her breast, very large and very soft, in one hard hand and squeezed harder and she cried out, wrapping her arms around him and clutching him to her.

Fargo broke off the kiss and allowed his tongue to trace a path down her throat and across her chest. He found her nipple and sucked on it, pulling it into his mouth. Ophelia cupped the back of his head and rumpled his mane of black hair, holding him tight against her breast.

He ran his hand over the slightly rounded belly and into the thick thatch of her pubic hair. He found the place he wanted but she was still dry.

Fargo nibbled her tits and continued to finger her. He squirmed lower and probed her navel with the tip of his tongue, then rested his chin in the curly bush and flicked the tiny button alternately with finger and tongue. The fluids began to gather and seep. Slowly she became as moist and ready as a young girl.

Ophelia's hips were pumping in earnest now, and she was kneading the back of his head with insistent strength. He continued patiently until Ophelia was fully receptive and on until her full, lush body jerked and shuddered in a powerful climax.

Then, deliberately brusque, she pushed him onto his back. "My turn," she said decisively, and bent to him, pulling him deep into the heat of her grasping mouth. She sucked him deep into her mouth and began to bob her head swiftly up and down, her full red lips pressed tight around his shaft.

Fargo held back, putting off the pleasure of his own climax as she continued driving herself down onto him, darting up and down now with an almost frantic speed.

He could feel her breasts lift and swing with her efforts, feeling the weight of them on his stomach every time she moved herself down onto him, their warmth pulling away from him with every rapid withdrawal.

The pressures in his groin rose, threatening to fill his balls and burst them like a balloon. Fargo held back until he could resist no more. With a gush of sweet, almost unbearably acute pleasure, he let go, a hot stream of pale fluid spewing out of him.

Ophelia's mouth stayed on him until he was completely satisfied. Then she finally released him as he relaxed, limp and spent in every fiber of his lean frame.

Ophelia pulled away, licking the sticky residue from her lips.

"That was wonderful," she said.

"I agree," Fargo told her. He pulled her on top of him so her huge breasts were pressing against his chest. "I could enjoy that every night," he said. Ophelia smiled. "But won't Miss Loy get suspicious if you quit using the tent?"

"She won't say anything," Ophelia said.

"Good," Fargo responded. He rolled sideways so they were once again lying face to face. He found one soft brown nipple and teased it erect by rolling it between his thumb and forefinger, then reached down to her crotch. Ophelia parted her thighs to receive him. She was still wet and welcoming there.

"Surely you can't . . . not already . . .?"

"Try me," he said.

Obediently she reached for him. She gasped with surprise and pleasure to find him hard and ready again.

4

"Damn," Fargo blurted.

The dark shapes materialized through the white curtain of blowing snow. There were a half a dozen of them or more. They were a hundred twenty five yards or so out and moving closer on foot.

Obviously someone in that crowd knew about this huge, sheltering rock formation. Sometime during the night they had figured out where the Porter Players were apt to be, and now they were moving in.

For a kill? Fargo wondered. He still couldn't be sure of their intentions. The Sharps came to his shoulder, but he held his fire. They hadn't yet actually displayed any hostile intentions. But dammit. . . .

The pursuers had seen him now.

And so much for questionable intentions.

A flash of yellow flame flickered in the early-morning light as one of the men fired at him. The rush of the wind whipped away the sound of the gunshot. But there was no doubt now that these folks were getting serious.

Fargo's finger tightened on the trigger of the Sharps, and the stubby weapon boomed hollowly as it recoiled against his shoulder.

Out in front of him the nearest of the men—there were seven of them, he could see now—spun and fell as a five-hundred-grain lead bullet tore through the man's right side.

Fargo cursed. He had held his sights dead-center on the rifleman's chest, but the force of the wind had drifted the bullet that far left in just the short distance the slug had to travel. Long-range sniping with any degree of accuracy wasn't going to be possible in this kind of wind.

In front of him, all of the men disappeared, throwing themselves down into the snow and out of Fargo's line of sight.

Behind him, Porter and his people heard the report of the Sharps and flung themselves into swift, efficient motion.

Fargo looked toward them and was pleased. Damn near any other group of dudes he had ever guided would have been caught cold by the early-morning approach. But these actors and actresses were always ready for an early trail. And now that there was definitely a need for speed, they produced it.

Lofton and Croft began yanking cinches tight. The women abandoned the breakfast fire, Ophelia taking time to dump the coffeepot and skillet and tie the utensils to the strings on her saddle. Amon Porter dashed first for their precious script and makeup cases, then began to gather already rolled bedding and to lash the bundles onto the packsaddles. The group was wasting neither time nor motion, Fargo saw.

Something plucked at Fargo's left sleeve, and he glanced down to see a jagged tear opened in the cloth of his coat by a bullet. He hadn't even heard the shot.

He threw the Sharps back to his shoulder and fired into a snowdrift behind which someone could have been hiding. The fact that he neither saw nor heard any response meant nothing. Quickly he reloaded again and cocked the Sharps. The players were doing just fine with the preparations for leaving. It was up to the Trailsman to keep the gunmen at bay.

He crouched and ran to his right, to the shelter of the boulder where he had slept. Catherine Loy darted up behind him, bent, grabbed his bedroll, and raced away.

Something—a hat or a head—was briefly visible out front.

The Sharps came to Fargo's shoulder. He aimed a good foot to the right of his target to compensate for the wind drift and touched off the shot.

Fargo chuckled softly to himself. It had been a hat, not a head. The bullet from the Sharps struck the crown and sent the hat flying. The wind caught it and sent it downwind at high speed, like a bird sailing through the air.

Before Fargo could reload, two figures popped into view long enough to trigger shots in his direction. He ducked behind his boulder and never knew where the bullets went.

"We're ready when you are." It was Croft who was speaking to him. The man had come up practically to his shoulder without him being able to hear the approach.

"Go ahead and get mounted, all of you," Fargo said. "I'll be along in a moment."

Croft nodded and ran back toward the waiting horses.

Fargo crouched and, Sharps at the ready, leaned out

from the protection of the boulder. There were three men upright and moving in.

He sent them scurrying for cover with an unaimed snap shot from his Sharps.

"Good enough," he told himself as he ran for the horses, fingers racing to reload the Sharps as he moved.

He vaulted onto the saddle of the pinto and gathered his reins. "Come on," he shouted.

Fargo led out, from the shelter of the monolith and into the gale force of the blowing snow, taking the party north toward Poncha Pass.

He hated having to be in the lead of the party now, with armed men left behind. But neither Porter nor any of the others seemed capable of choosing the path they were going to have to take today, and it would take entirely too much time to try to explain it to them. Fargo had to lead. There was no choice about it if they were going to slip away from this crowd, especially since at least one member of that bunch knew this country or they wouldn't have showed up here for a morning ambush. Damn them.

Fargo pushed the pinto only for the first few hundred yards. That was enough. Visibility was less than a hundred and fifty yards. The men who had been setting up the ambush had left their horses somewhere behind. When Fargo had seen them, they were on foot. So, even if they had left their horses reasonably close, they would lose time running back for their mounts.

Fargo thought rapidly as he rode, the Porter Players bunched close behind the tail of the Ovaro.

Wherever those men had spent the night, their horses probably wouldn't be entirely fresh now. And once again, particularly in these conditions, endurance was going to make a hell of a lot of difference—much more so than simple speed. He reined back on the pinto, letting the animal drop back to a pace that would cover ground without sapping too much of the horse's strength.

The trick now, he reasoned, would be to lose the pursuit.

The men who were behind them knew good and well that they'd been pointing for Poncha ever since they left Taos. That was obvious, or they wouldn't have come all the way north to the monolith. If they'd been tricked into heading for Wolf Creek, they never would've come this far.

With any damned luck at all now, the pursuers would keep on into Poncha, Fargo hoped.

Fargo's face was grim when he thought about what might happen to those men if they tried Poncha now.

With or without pursuit, though, his intention had been to turn away from that mountain pass this morning.

Yesterday, until the storm resumed, he would have been willing to try the pass, but not after a full night of blizzard conditions and with more blowing snow to come.

By now the pass that made it possible to cross the mountains would be drifted full of dense snow. The same break that formed the pass would also act as a perfect catch basin for deep drifts. And after this much snow, the road could be under twenty feet of snow or more. They were going to have to turn aside anyway. With luck, those pursuers would keep on, though.

Fargo shuddered. If those poor bastards got caught in the drifts. . . . He wouldn't wish that on anyone.

He glanced over his shoulder. There was nothing but white behind the party. No sign whatsoever of the pursuit. Satisfied, he shoved the Sharps back into its scabbard and reached for the welcome protection of his buffalo-hide gauntlet. In the few minutes his hands had been exposed they felt numb. He hunkered lower inside his coat and guided the pinto with care.

His eyes kept darting to the side, to the right searching for the exact conditions he needed.

They were still following exposed hillsides, riding in the full force of the wind so the horses would have easier going. And so there would be no telltale tracks left behind to show the pursuers that they had come this way. Even with wind and snow this bad, there would be windswept dimples left behind for half an hour or longer if they were to buck directly through any of the drifts. And Fargo didn't want to risk that.

So he rode north, leading his group away from the direction he intended to take them, until at last they tilted down a slight slope and found a bare patch of ground leading off to the right. With a grunt of satisfaction, Fargo turned the pinto and followed it, riding east now.

He led them only a few yards in that direction, though, then doubled back and took them south, forcing through the hock-deep snow beside a wind-carved line of deep drift.

"What the hell are we doing?"

Fargo could barely hear Amon Porter's angry voice even though the man shouted.

"False trail," Fargo yelled back.

The group trudged along in Skye Fargo's footsteps. They rode south for a short distance, then turned east again, lining out directly across a flat expanse of deep snow.

The men following behind would be sticking with the windswept bare sections, Fargo was sure. They would be pushing their horses as hard as they thought they dared. They wouldn't take the time to explore every possible turnout, especially when they were convinced that they knew where the Porter Players were going.

So it should be safe enough to leave tracks here, until they could reach another line of bare earth and go south again.

Hell, by now the gunmen might already have passed the spot where Fargo had turned off.

In half an hour, Fargo thought, to forty-five minutes, and there won't be any more tracks for them to follow even if they did figure it out.

They reached a bare hilltop and Fargo turned south again, then later east.

They were crossing another barren white flat when the pinto suddenly dropped out from under Fargo, plunging down an unseen, snow-filled embankment.

Icy water splashed onto Fargo's legs and boots, chilling him instantly.

A lesser rider would have been unseated, but Fargo's unthinking balance, moving always in concert with the pinto that had served him so well for so very long, kept him in the saddle. As it was, he grabbed his horn and pushed, managing to avoid a nasty crash of his face with the back of the pinto's head when the horse came to an abrupt stop at the bottom of the embankment.

It stood there, chest-deep in snow and with its legs in flowing creek water. The stout horse shook itself like a wet dog, then with a plunging, porpoiselike series of lunges forced its way across the creek and up the other bank.

The players behind him, warned by Fargo's sudden disappearance, picked their way more carefully across the creek.

"Are you sure you know where we are, Mr. Fargo?" Porter asked when they were all across.

"We'll be in some trees in half an hour, Mr. Porter. We'll stop for the night there."

"Do you think it wise to stop so early?" Porter asked.

Fargo looked at the trembling horse Porter rode. The Ovaro was still in fair shape, even though it had been breaking trail for the others for the better part of eight hours. The other horses, coarser bred, were already shaky.

"The horses need a rest, unless you'd like to walk to Taos," Fargo said.

Porter blanched and turned his head away.

Didn't think so, Fargo muttered to himself.

"Come on," he said aloud. He kneed the pinto forward, moving with the wind again, moving east to the trees at the foot of the Sangre de Cristos.

The wind and snow were blowing as hard now as they had been all through last night and all during the day.

Fargo glanced over his left shoulder. There was nothing to see there, of course, but he couldn't help worrying. If those poor sons of bitches who had been following them were really up there in Poncha, God pity them. Because no one and nothing else would show them any mercy.

The storm roared across the flat sweep of the San Luis Valley for two more days before it finally blew itself out. In that time Skye Fargo was able to lead his party of thespians no more than thirty miles, a distance they would have covered in less than a day if conditions had been better. On the morning of the third day Fargo swirled the grounds of his coffee in the bottom of his cup and tossed them aside with a flick of his wrist.

"Time we get moving," he said. Obediently the Porter Players began to gather up the last of the gear and move toward the horses.

"What I figure," Fargo said to no one in particular, "is that today we'd better angle south a ways. There's a settlement I know of but haven't actually rode through yet. Fort Garland, I think it is."

"No," Porter said quickly.

"These animals need grain, man. We've used about all you packed. They need the grain. And unless Miss Margot has all of a sudden forgot how to make coffee, I'm betting we need some other things too. We've got to eat and so does the stock."

"We can't chance it," Porter said. "Those men—"

"Those men are way the hell behind. If they didn't die in Poncha Pass, they likely headed west toward Wolf Creek. There wasn't any hint that we'd turned east, because they know from where they last saw us that they'd have had to cross our trail for us to do that. Likely they won't see any way we could've with all the snow on the ground."

Fargo handed his empty cup to Catherine Loy and stood, stretching. He pulled his gauntlets on and surveyed the silent white world that lay unbroken by color for as far as the eye could see. The sky was still leaden and low, and a little snow continued to drift down from the clouds, although mercifully now without the driving force of the wind behind it.

"We can't take the chance—"

"What we can't do," Fargo interrupted, "is try to make it over La Veta Pass without food."

"You can shoot all the food we need," Porter protested. "Surely now that the storm is over, the game will be coming out again."

Fargo shook his head in disgust at the unthinking selfishness of the man. "First," he said, "we don't know for sure that the storm *is* over. That wind can come up again any time it takes a notion to. But more than that, Porter, I won't allow any stock under my care to starve to death. No matter what you think, I can't go out and shoot down a hundredweight of oats or a bag of barley."

Porter frowned.

"Amon," Ophelia said in a low, warning tone.

"Yes?"

She shook her head, and he reluctantly dropped his protests.

"Thank you," Fargo told her.

She nodded and winked at him. Not three hours earlier she had vacated his bedroll. She had every right to be exhausted, but she gave no indication of that.

Since Ophelia Margot began sharing his bed, Fargo had not seen much of Catherine Loy. The younger woman had even taken to riding at the tail of their procession when they were in motion. When they were in camp, she avoided him. Apparently, unless she had taken up with Croft or Lofton, she was spending her nights in the company of the makeup case.

The men finished the chore of loading the mules and

lashing the last of the gear into place. As usual, Porter tied the script satchel behind his saddle while Ophelia took charge of the makeup bag.

Funny, Fargo thought suspiciously how the woman never seemed to worry all that much about the makeup freezing during the day when the bag was tied behind her cantle. It certainly had been a helluva long time since they had seen temperatures, day or night, that broke above the freezing point.

"Let's go," he said, dismissing his suspicion for the moment, and one by one they fell into line behind the Ovaro's lead.

For the first time since they left the monolith, Fargo turned away from the scant protection of the Sangre de Cristos and headed across the broad, empty flats.

A foot or more of snow lay over the entire scope of the country, and the drifts were hat-deep to a man on horseback behind any vertical obstruction and in the cuts gouged by runoff water. Fargo had to pick their way carefully to avoid taking the animals into the strength-sapping drifts. At best the traveling was hard on them. Even the sturdy pinto was wearing down after days of travel with restricted grain rations. The break at Fort Garland was going to be necessary if they expected to get across La Veta safely.

Fargo had never been to that settlement, but he had been told roughly where it was. And that would be enough, he was confident.

When they stopped for lunch, Porter glanced nervously toward Ophelia, then approached Fargo. As usual, the two actors were off by themselves, engaged in low, private conversation. Fargo wondered what those two could have to talk about so damned much.

"I, uh, I wanted to ask you about this fort you say we are going to."

"It's not a fort," Fargo said. "Not anymore, though they tell me there were troops there once."

"No troops?"

"Uh-huh."

Porter seemed to relax a little.

The Trailsman's eyes narrowed. "Why is that important to you, Porter?"

"What?"

"When I told you there weren't any troops at Fort Garland, you got an easier look about you. So why's it mean something to you? Why don't you want to see any brass buttons?"

The old man looked embarrassed. He looked around to make sure no one else was listening. "I—you will keep this confidential, won't you?"

"Likely," Fargo said, not quite promising, but coming as close to it as he was willing until he heard Porter's story.

Porter moved a step closer and lowered his voice. "When we were in Santa Fe, I had, uh, a minor dispute with a captain of dragoons."

"The army likes to call them cavalry these days," Fargo said.

"Yes, well, the, uh, falling out concerned a certain"—he looked around again and licked his lips. The man was practically squirming. "It was about a lady of the evening. A soiled dove, if you know what I mean. The matter was resolved without recourse to violence, I assure you. I, uh, outbid him, as it were. But there were loud recriminations and certain threats made. And you see, sir, I have no idea where the, uh,

87

gentleman might be stationed. I was afraid that if he were posted to this Fort Garland place, well. . . ."

Fargo chuckled. "Don't worry about it," he assured the old dandy. "There aren't any troopers at Garland. You won't run into the guy there."

Porter exhaled loudly. "Thank you. You relieve my mind greatly."

"Sure."

Porter turned and walked briskly back to the others, his shoulders square and his step jaunty again.

Fargo couldn't help laughing to himself about the old boy's fears. He was encouraged by them, to tell the truth. If a man of Amon Porter's age was still getting into woman trouble, he couldn't be all bad.

Fargo chuckled softly to himself while he finished his cold meal.

Hot food would be a welcome treat tonight, he reflected as he ate. Cooking fires were no danger any longer, with those gunmen far behind. But they had been unable to find any wood or even dried dung to build a noon fire with. Everything was too deeply covered with snow. They likely wouldn't find fuel again until they returned to the timber at the foot of La Veta.

After lunch they climbed stiffly back into their saddles and again began breaking snow.

The settlement of Fort Garland announced itself to him late in the afternoon. A thin column of gray smoke pinpointed an outlying farm or ranch. Beyond it he could see a number of similar columns. The source of all those smokes would surely be the town.

Fargo aimed the nose of the Ovaro toward the smoke. He glanced behind him, toward the west. There was a solid cloud cover so that he couldn't see the sun. But if his reckoning was accurate, they should get to Fort Garland just about dark—he smiled to himself—just in time for a hot dinner.

The pinto seemed to sense Fargo's quickened interest. The horse's ears flicked back and forth, and it tossed its head impatiently. Without its master's direction, the Ovaro picked up the pace to a long-striding fast walk despite the depth of the snow it was having to break, and it pulled slightly on the bit. Fargo leaned forward in his saddle and stroked the horse's neck.

"Soon," he promised. "You'll get you a good rub-down and a quiet stall out of the wind and the cold. And I'll buy you a damn gallon of oats and maybe some corn to mix into it, eh?"

He had no idea that he wouldn't keep those words.

5

The buildings at the west end of the town—there were
not very many of them—were a welcome sight with the
promise of warmth and comfort showing in the glow of
lamplight coming from their windows. It was nearly
dark and people had already begun to light their lamps
in preparation for the night. Fargo could see a high,
blocky roof that had to be the settlement's livery barn.
He raised up in his stirrups, got Porter's attention, and
pointed toward the shelter.

As he did so, there was a fiery yellow blossom that
flared in the twilight and quickly after it the sound of a
rifle shot.

The slug snarled past between Fargo and Amon Porter, zipping through with a nasty, sizzling sort of
sound.

Fargo wheeled the pinto to his left and shouted,
"Ambush, dammit. Line out."

Within seconds the first shot was followed by a ragged volley of others. Two, four, five more shots. Once
the first fool had let go, they all opened up. One of the
mules squealed, and Catherine Loy's horse began to jit-
ter and jump.

"Move, dammit!"

Fargo pulled his Colt and leveled it in the general direction of the big barn. The distance was too great, well over a hundred yards, for him to do any damage. But he could damn sure make the shooters think. He fired twice, held up while the Porter Players blew past him, then emptied the revolver in the direction of the barn.

If one of those bastards hadn't been so itchy to start the ball rolling and if they'd waited until the outfit was in the street so they couldn't miss . . . Fargo didn't want to think about the results. It would've been raw hell, with hot, fresh blood steaming in the snow.

He holstered the Colt and spurred the pinto in behind the dudes, who were at a hard gallop. Snow thrown by the churning hooves of their spooked horses flew up like a cloud, like a miniature ground blizzard, which helped to hide them from the gunmen who were being left behind.

There were some more rifle shots from the edge of the town, but Fargo heard no more bullets.

The fast-moving pinto quickly caught up with the others, and Fargo swept around them to guide them in a sweeping curve that would carry them around the settlement to the north and on toward La Veta Pass. There was no sense in worrying about tracks now. The ambushers already knew where they were headed. The only question was how fast the gunmen could get mounted and begin the pursuit.

Fargo heard a shout from behind his shoulder. He hauled back on his reins, bringing the Ovaro to a sliding stop in a flurry of thrown snow.

Amon Porter was down, his horse was on its knees, struggling to regain its feet. Behind it, the first mule was dead, and the lead rope tied to it had brought down Porter's horse. Apparently one of the slugs had found a target.

"Shit," Fargo muttered. He wheeled the pinto back and yelled for the others to go on. "Half a mile and stop. Wait for us."

They dashed past, Lofton in the lead, while Fargo grabbed for his knife.

Someone behind them had damned good eyesight in the poor light. A rifle cracked. The slug kicked snow twenty yards in front of the struggling Porter, then ricocheted off the frozen ground. Another of the mules let out a startled bray.

Fargo hauled the Ovaro in tight beside the downed horse and leaned out of his saddle with the knife flashing in his fist.

Another rifle fired behind him, and the bullet whined by not a foot from his head.

He slashed quickly at the lead rope. The fibers resisted for a moment, then parted, letting the frantic horse free from the drag of the dead mule.

The horse lurched to its feet, nearly unseating Porter and bashing into Fargo's right leg as it scrambled upright.

"Go," Fargo shouted. He dragged his Sharps from its scabbard and held the carbine like a pistol for a one-handed shot behind him. He knew damn well he wouldn't hit anything back there, but he wanted to discourage the riflemen. "Go," he shouted again. Porter hadn't moved. He sat on his trembling horse with an uncomprehending look on his face.

"But the packs . . ." Porter protested.

Fargo didn't bother to answer. Couldn't the silly son

of a bitch see that one of the mules was dead and at least one other wounded? If they waited around to worry about a bunch of damned gear, there would likely be people dead too. He jumped the pinto up behind Porter's horse and cracked the animal on the rump with the ends of his reins. The horse took off, carrying a protesting Porter with it. The Ovaro thundered close behind. The retreat was punctuated by another crackle of gunfire from behind.

They caught up with the others about three quarters of a mile out, and Fargo pulled the whole crowd to a halt. "Is everybody all right?"

They all tried to answer at once.

"Whoa. One at a time. Miss Loy?" He pointed at her and waited for an answer. She turned her face shyly away from his but nodded that she was unhurt.

"Miss Margot?"

"Undamaged but rather out of breath, I confess."

"You two?" Croft and Lofton nodded.

Fargo didn't ask the question of Porter. Instead he dismounted and checked for himself to see that Porter's horse had not suffered any real harm from its fall.

"Where are the mules? All our things?" Croft asked.

Fargo hooked a thumb over his shoulder, in the direction of Fort Garland.

"You simply must go back and get them," Croft said.

The man was beginning to grate on Fargo. It was nothing he could really pin down, but Croft's voice seemed to carry a thin hint of snotty whine to it under deep and cultured professional tones.

Fargo ignored him. He completed his examination of Porter's horse, then remounted the pinto. "I don't know if that was the same crowd we've seen before. Maybe, maybe not. It doesn't really matter. What does matter is that they know where we're headed now. They've had time to get their horses, and their mounts are likely to be fresh and rested. They got grain for their horses; we don't. Any direction we want to go, we'll leave a trail a blind child could follow. So I really think that losing those damn pack mules is one of our smaller troubles.''

"What . . . what can we do?" It was Catherine who asked the question they all wanted to pose. Her voice was very small.

The Trailsman shrugged and grinned. ''We'll do what we can. Now let's go.'' He walked the pinto around into the lead of the group and pointed the horse toward where he thought La Veta Pass should be. A silent and very subdued group of thespians fell in behind his lead.

Fargo held them up when they reached the first of the trees, at the foot of the rising hills that would lead to La Veta. He could as easily have stopped at any other spot. It would be dangerously foolish to build a fire, even if they had had anything to cook. They didn't need shelter on the windless night except from the cold, and there was no escape from that in any direction, barring the warmth of a fire. Yet he knew that the nearness of the living trees would give them a comfort in the mind if not in the body, so he halted the group there.

"Pull your saddles and give the horses a rub, then put the saddles back on in case we have to move in a hurry,'' he instructed. He singled out the younger men. ''As soon as you get your saddles back on, scrounge for anything eatable.''

"I haven't a gun,'' Lofton said.

"Not for us. For the horses. Pull grass if you can find any under the spread of these pines, cottonwood bark if you run into any of that. Anything that looks like a horse can eat it, you drag it back here."

"All right." Lofton accepted the instruction cheerfully enough. Croft scowled but said nothing.

"What shall we do?" Ophelia asked.

"Tend your horses. Then let them be. They need some rest." Fargo worked quickly to take care of the pinto, then reset his saddle and pulled the Sharps from its boot. He walked away from the group and hunkered in the snow, watching the black and gray outlines of their back trail in the night. He wouldn't move the group until he had to. The only question he had now was not whether there was someone coming after them but how far behind.

He waited there for nearly three quarters of an hour before he heard anything. Then a faint sound reached him out of the darkness, carrying crisp and clear on the still, cold air. It was a thin, bell-like tinkle. Someone back there used chain on his bits, chain to weight his reins or as a curb. Fargo turned his head and spoke softly over his shoulder.

"Time to move. Pull your cinches, then get on real quiet and slip off in the direction we've been heading. The flat of the road's plain enough. Follow it."

"What about you?" The voice was a whisper, probably Porter's.

"I'll be along. Don't worry. I can't lose your tracks any more than they can. You lead, Mr. Porter. Then the ladies. Then the other men behind. Just go the way I told you. Take it nice and easy. We don't want to use up the horses if we don't have to. Every fifteen minutes, somebody else take the lead. That way none of the animals has to break all the trail. Can you do that?''

"Yes." Porter sounded frightened. Fargo was aware of some whispering among the members of the group, but none of them said anything that he could make out.

"Go on now. Quiet as you can.''

"All right.''

He heard them go, no noisier than he'd expected by now.

He felt better once they were out of the way. Whatever happened to them was his responsibility. At least this way none of them would be hit by a stray bullet.

Fargo closed his eyes and tilted his head to the side, concentrating on listening. Whoever was coming, however many of them there were, they were too far away to see yet. But he was beginning to be able to hear them more clearly now. Frequently the metallic *p-ting* of the chain on bit steel floated to his ears, and once a low snort of fright from a horse. Likely the animal had stumbled, he figured. Fargo opened his eyes again.

There were dark shapes moving, dimly seen against the gray of the snow blanket. Moonlight, even starlight, overhead would have made them easy targets, but there was still a layer of cloud between the ground and the stars.

Fargo held a gauntleted hand over the action of the Sharps and eased the hammer back, not wanting the sound to reach the men, who were perhaps a hundred seventy-five yards in front of and slightly below his position. He cocked the Sharps and dropped the gauntlet from his right hand onto the snow at his side.

Carefully, taking his time, he dropped back into a sitting position in the snow. The cold of it reached his butt through his jeans when he wriggled lower, compacting the snow and making a solid seat for himself. He rested his left elbow in front of his knee, careful not to connect bone with bone and thus make his rest less steady. He drew in a breath, released half of it, and dipped his head to his sights.

There was so little light that he had to square his sights against the snow, then swing on line with the lead rider.

They were closer now. He could make out the figures of the riders and horses. There were five of them. Again he wondered if these might be the same men, or some of them, who had been on them before. He had no way to tell.

His finger closed on the trigger, taking up the slack against the sear until the weapon was ready to fire at the slightest additional pressure.

A twitch, a touch, and the lead rider would'be dead.

Fargo swore to himself.

No sane man would be out on a night like this. There was no chance at all. But what if these were not the gunmen who had tried to shoot them? What if this was some other party, travelers from Taos trying to get to El Pueblo, maybe? What if the hired gunmen sent by Wickse, Porter's competitor, were five minutes behind this bunch?

Fargo had no sympathy at all for any son of a bitch that took a shot at him. But, dammit, he wasn't long on the idea of gunning down any passing stranger who happened to be in a tough place at the wrong time.

"Damn," he muttered.

The muzzle of the Sharps drooped lower by a fraction of an inch as Fargo readjusted his aim.

Then the last fraction of an ounce of pressure was applied to the trigger of the Sharps.

The gun bellowed and spat fire. The bullet hit the first horse, which screamed in pain and reared, dumping its rider into the snow and falling over backward with its legs thrashing. Fargo hated like hell to hit an innocent animal, but right about now he was running out of choices.

The echo of the muzzle blast had not died away before Fargo was on his feet, spinning away from the place where his muzzle flash would have been seen. He crouched and scuttled sideways, fingers racing to reload the Sharps as he moved.

He stopped and raised the gun. It was too dark for him to see for sure, but it looked like there was a hell of a storm going on down there. The men were shouting and the frightened horses were rearing, and no one paying any attention to the hillside where Fargo was.

Finally one of them regained enough control to pound an answering shot in the direction of Fargo's original position. The man was not a bad shot. Even under such poor shooting conditions, Fargo could see snow fly within a couple feet of where he had just been.

He took careful aim again. This time Fargo sighted down his barrel toward a more or less empty area in the midst of the melee that was going on down there. He fired again, the flame from his muzzle lighting the surface of the snow for fifteen feet in all directions. The slug hit nothing, but then he had not intended it to. He still wasn't sure if these were the bunch after them, and wanted only to stir them up a bit.

As soon as he had fired he whirled and raced away to a new location.

This time three of them returned his fire.

"You cocksucker." The shout came across the snow clearly.

The men, whoever they were, were angry, but they weren't stupid. Trading shots with someone who could see you but not be seen himself with the dark backdrop of the evergreens behind him was a losing proposition, and each of them had to know it. The man whose horse had been shot was dragged up behind the cantle of one of the others, and the bunch turned tail and fogged it back the way they'd come. They were out of Fargo's sight before they had gone two hundred yards.

Fargo nodded with satisfaction and then returned to the same spot where he'd first waited for the pursuers to catch up.

He'd wait a half an hour, he figured, pulling his gauntlet back on his chilled right hand. If the bunch had been discouraged enough to run back to Fort Garland, another half-hour wouldn't do any harm. And if they were going to come again, they would figure he'd be on his horse and moving by then. They wouldn't expect him to be waiting for them in a second ambush.

Fargo sat and waited.

It didn't take half an hour. Within fifteen minutes he could see the men returning. They came on slowly now and were quieter than they'd been. They rode spread out now and quite certainly had their rifles held at the ready.

Fargo watched them come. As they passed the spot where he'd first fired at them, he stood and slipped back into the protection of a tree trunk. He braced his left arm against the side of the trunk to give himself a firm rest and took very careful aim at the chest of the horse that was now leading.

The horse went down at his shot and, predictably, the air of both sides was cut by bullets as the men tried to catch him changing positions.

Instead Fargo stayed where he was long enough to see the group, now five men mounted on three horses, charge belly-down through the deep snow in a run for safety.

The Trailsman threw one final shot over their heads, then headed for the waiting pinto.

They'd wait till daylight if they had the nerve to come again at all. And if they did move again, it would damn sure be slow and cautious.

That was exactly what Fargo wanted. With any kind of luck at all he could have his group across La Veta before any pursuit could reach them.

6

"Damn you. Don't you people have any sense?" Fargo shook his head in disgust. "Never mind answering that. I can see that you don't, not a one of you."

The men glowered back at him. Catherine Loy put a pout on her pretty face. Only Ophelia Margot seemed unaffected by Fargo's tirade. She was busy building a fire.

Fargo continued to shake his head. He pointed. "Look at them. Don't you know better than to push horses like that?"

The horses, hard-pressed for speed on an uphill climb in deep, unbroken snow, were sweaty and trembling with utter exhaustion. Fargo had caught up with the fleeing actors almost two-thirds of the way up the climb to the pass. And he had managed to catch up to them then only because they had come to a forced halt when two of the horses refused to travel any farther.

"Put the saddles back on them," Fargo snapped. "Sweaty as they are, in weather like this, they've to be cooled down before you pull those blankets." He pointed at the two younger men. "Take the reins of all of them and walk them. Keep them going in slow circles till they cool off some. And mind you stay out in front of them to break the crust. The rest of you can go on foot and find some forage for them to eat.''

Miss Loy's pout became more pronounced, but at the moment Fargo did not give a shit. The prospect of finding himself up here with a bunch of unhorsed dudes was not attractive.

"What about our fire?" Ophelia asked quietly.

"The fire can wait. It'll be a spell before us humans get to warm up." He glared. "Thanks to all of you."

"Really now—" Porter began.

One flashing look from Fargo's ice-blue eyes was enough to quiet the man. Porter flushed a bright pink and turned away from the confrontation before it could develop. The Trailsman was damn well ready to turn away from this crowd and leave them there, and Porter could see the hair-trigger edge Fargo was balanced on.

Lofton and Croft gathered up the reins of the sweaty horses and began to lead the patient beasts in slow circles in the broken snow near the camp they had been trying to establish when Fargo found them. The others, including both women, stumbled off into the trees in search of dried grasses they could gather from beneath the protective covering of the evergreens.

When they were gone, Fargo, still muttering to himself, tended to the pinto. At least the Ovaro was still in fairly decent condition. Even after Fargo had realized what the fools ahead of him were doing, how fast they were pushing their mounts through the night after a full day of hard use, he had refused to rush the pinto in an effort to catch up to them. If anyone was going to become stranded and left afoot in this white wilderness, it was not going to be Skye Fargo.

Now he pulled his saddle and felt under the blanket

for excessive sweat before he removed the blanket from the pinto's back. Immediately, before the sturdy horse could begin to feel the effects of the sudden cold on its back, he took up a handful of dried needles and ground litter and used that to give the horse a thorough, invigorating rubdown.

Catherine Loy returned to the camp before he was done. She was carrying a few scant handfuls of grass stems. "Here," she said.

"That's not enough," Fargo told her. "We need forage by the armload. Go back and do a proper job this time."

It was another hour and a half, and a new dawn was past, before the last of the horses was finally cooled down and rubbed dry and there was enough forage piled in front of them for Fargo to relent and let the humans rest. He allowed Ophelia to finish making her fire and called them all around the blaze.

"Now look," he told them. "You people don't know enough about these mountains to be scared of them the way a sensible person ought. So let me tell you something. Forget about those yahoos that are trying to shoot at you. That sort of thing I can protect you from. What I can't save you from is your own stupidity. Up here your horse is the most valuable thing you've got, because it's the welfare of that horse that's going to make the difference between whether you live to go down the other side of that pass or stay here till the spring thaw.

"You can die up here," Fargo continued. "You could freeze to death or get yourself buried in a snow slide or walk out on a ledge of corniced snow and fall five hundred feet. There's all manners of ways you can kill yourselves around here, and any one of them will kill you stone-dead, and the corpse will be frozen stiff inside a couple hours. Now, do you all understand what I'm saying?''

No one replied. The Porter Players just sat on a pair of dead logs Fargo had dragged up close to the fire, with their eyes down and their hands clasped like a bunch of unruly schoolchildren catching it from teacher.

"All I'm gonna add is this," Fargo went on. "If you folks keep thinking that you're more important than your horses, you'll find yourselves on your own up here. And if that happens, I doubt there'll be two of you that lives to see bare ground again."

Fargo looked around at the stark white hell that surrounded them. He smelled the air, his nostril hairs froze and felt like small, sharp spikes inside his nose. Every step he took was in snow that squeaked with dry, bitter cold.

"We don't have any instruments with us," he said, "but right now the temperature is probably ten, twenty degrees below zero. I didn't say below freezing, folks. I said below zero. So if you think you can walk out through this, go right ahead. I sure as hell won't stop you. But I won't tote your body down for burial either. That'll be your own problem."

He looked at the booted feet sticking out from under the coats and capes of the troupe members. "I don't suppose any of you was smart enough to fetch along moccasins instead of those boots?"

Croft and Ophelia shook their heads. The others didn't bother, although their answers were obviously the same.

"I didn't think so, and that's a pity. Mocs and

Indian-style leggings have some give to them. They let your foot flex and keep the circulation going. Boots get cold. So what you're going to have to do from now on is stop every couple hours to build a fire, take your boots off, and dry and warm your feet. No exceptions. You understand me?''

This time they all nodded.

"That's the only way to avoid frostbite. You keep your feet dry and warm, and maybe you can walk out of here alive.''

"Walk?" Porter asked, and Fargo took in the startled glances of them all.

"That's what I said. Walk. You already just about ruined those horses. And all they got to eat up here is snow, and it won't get any better for them till we get down the other side. So from here on, you'll have to walk and lead your horses.''

"What about food for us?''

"If I find anything, which will be tough this time of year, I'll fetch us in some meat. Otherwise, we pull our belts tighter and make do. Now, all of you, take those boots off and get your feet warm and dry. We're fixing to leave out of here in just a couple minutes.''

"Don't the horses need to rest?''

"They'll be able to tough it out as long as nobody tries to ride them the rest of the way. You took advantage of those animals, so now you have to pay the price.''

Shaking his head again, Fargo resaddled the Ovaro and got a pair of high-topped, fringed moccasins from his saddlebags. He exchanged the mocs and a set of blanket leggings for his boots and pulled on his gauntlets.

"Come on," he said.

"Shall I put out the fire?" Ophelia asked.

Fargo shook his head. "Leave it. It won't cause a runaway fire with all this snow on the ground. And if anybody's coming up the trail after you, it'll make them think you're still here. Might make them cautious and slow them down some if they think there could be a rifleman still in the woods close by."

"All right."

Fargo swung into the saddle of the pinto. He cheerfully ignored the dirty looks he got when the others had to take their reins in their hands and lead their tired horses through the knee-deep snow.

After all, he wasn't the one who had been damn fool enough to jade his own mount in this kind of country. Besides, he would be getting plenty of work before this day was out, what with breaking trail and trying to cover their backsides at the same damn time. He and the pinto would damn sure earn their keep.

He spoke softly to the horse and headed slowly up the snow-blanketed trail toward the top of the pass.

The Trailsman let them rest when they reached the top of the pass, even though it was only late afternoon and there were still several hours of daylight remaining.

"You folks and those horses need rest now," he said. "Anyway, you're due for another foot warming."

"Should we remove the saddles?"

Fargo looked first toward the sky, which was still low and gray but not as solidly overcast as it had been since the snow stopped, then down along the back trail. There was no movement for as far as he could see, not even a puff of breeze stirring the snow-heavy branches. He nodded. "Pull them and turn the horses loose so they can paw through the snow for a bite or two of grass. They won't go anywhere in this stuff. Then go ahead and make yourselves a camp for the night. We all need some sleep."

"What about shelter? Our things were all on the mules," Lofton asked.

"You'll have to make do with the fire and saddle blankets. Buddy up and share the warmth. You'll do better if you make a heat reflector, but that's up to you, if you want to go through the work."

"And you?"

Fargo rubbed the pinto's muzzle, freeing it of the crust of ice that had formed from its own breathing. He turned the animal loose to forage for itself and picked up his bedroll and saddlebags. "I'll be up the hill there keeping an eye on the trail behind, in case somebody comes along."

"What about our supper?" Catherine asked.

Fargo shrugged and began to wade uphill through the snow. The surface was crusted hard and crisp. The depth was over his knees here.

"We're hungry," Croft protested.

Fargo paused long enough to grin at them. "They tell me leather is not so bad if you boil it long enough. Of course, I'd say you still need your boots, so first you might want to try any belts you think you can spare. Me, I'm not quite that hungry yet myself." He resumed his movement up the mountainside.

It was just as well, he thought, that he would not be in the camp this night. Testy as they all were, it would be constant bickering and complaining. With Skye Fargo as the butt of most of the complaints, unless he missed his mark badly. And what the hell, it might do them some good to get some of it out of their systems. They could do that better if he were not around anyway.

He took his time climbing the hillside above the flat V in the bottom of the pass, picking his way with care to avoid the deeper drifts and searching as he climbed for the spot he wanted.

Eventually he found a thick clump of spruce, a number of young trees growing close together, where the snow had largely been held on top of the branches and beyond the perimeter of the low canopy formed by the thick, evergreen foliage. Fargo propped his Sharps butt down in the deep snow, then dropped to his hands and knees and wriggled under the lowest branches. He found himself in a sheltered, pitlike area with snow piled to a depth of several feet all around.

Immediately under the trees, the ground was barely covered with white flakes that had managed to sift through the branches overhead. He broke off lower branches until he had an area large enough for him to sit up, then used the twigs like a broom to sweep away the snow and soggy needles until he had a dry and relatively warm nest where he could lay out his bedding.

When that was done, he sat up. Carefully trying not to dislodge too much more snow from above him, he used his knife to cut away more branches so that he had a small, clear tunnel down which he could watch the trail they had just traveled. If anyone was coming along behind them, he would be able to see from here.

He removed his boots and wriggled into his bedroll, draping the sougan and ground blanket over his shoulders like a cape so he could sit and watch in comfort until nightfall. The Sharps was at his side, his Colt in its holster.

There was nothing to do but wait and watch, but boredom wasn't a problem Skye Fargo was likely to suffer. He needed this time to think. And he had a great deal of thinking he wanted to do about this group of people known as the Porter Players. He had, of course, long since ceased congratulating himself on an easy-money job. Now he was wondering about them, in particular about Ophelia Margot.

Snow crunched under a boot to Fargo's left, downhill from where he sat. He grabbed up the Sharps and had it held at the ready almost before he had time to consciously register the fact that a sound had been heard.

It was almost as if his thoughts had brought the woman to him. There, trudging awkwardly along in the footsteps Fargo had recently made, was the buxon Miss Margot. She was panting from the exertion of the climb at this altitude. Her cheeks were a girlish red from the effects of exercise and extreme cold.

She stopped near the blank, green and white cone of the clump of spruce and in an uncertain voice asked, "Are you in there, Skye?"

"Nowhere else I could be, is there?"

"Oh." She sounded relieved. "May I join you?"

"Sure, why not? Be sure you come in from that side, though, same way I crawled in. And be careful you don't jiggle the branches. Knock the snow off the branches and anyone down below could see and figure there might be someone under here, and I don't want that."

"I'll be careful," she promised. She stamped around a little to break the snow down, then got on her stomach and wriggled inside the makeshift shelter. A look of amazement crossed her face when she saw him. "Why, this is quite cozy." She laughed. "I was beginning to believe I should't ever see bare earth again."

"Keep your voice down," Fargo said softly. "Loud noises are enough to drop snow as dry as this is."

"Of course." She crawled to his side and joined him inside his bedding.

"Fargo," Ophelia whispered.

He turned his head to look at her. The next thing he knew her mouth was locked hotly on his, her tongue probing between his lips.

He drew back from her a few inches and grinned. "Not a bad idea you had."

She smiled. "I told them I had to answer a call of nature. They shall draw the proper conclusion eventually, but frankly, dear, I don't care. Do you?"

"Not as long as you don't."

"I've never seen you in daylight before, she said. "Take your clothes off. Let me see as well as touch, my dear," she said with a coquettish laugh as she began undoing the buttons at the front of her dress.

Fargo shucked out of his clothes and pushed them down to the foot of the bedroll, where they would stay warm and dry, then helped her out of the last of her things.

Her body was full, which he already knew. In the good light he could see all of her at once for the first time, and the view was well worth some appreciation.

Her breasts were ripe and pale, her nipples a dusky, saddle brown and exceptionally large, surrounded by wrinkled plates of dark areolae. Her waist would have been large on a less full-bodied woman, but on her it was nipped in to form a classic hourglass shape above the round spread of her firm hips.

Ophelia took his erection in both hands, squeezing his shaft gently with one hand, while the other eased down to cup his balls, hefting them and tickling him with the sharp tips of her fingernails.

Fargo kissed her again, then dipped his head to suck one engorged nipple into his mouth. He pulled at her hungrily, drawing the nipple and as much of her breast as he could into his mouth. He sucked until his cheeks ached. Ophelia moaned with pleasure and began to stroke his cock faster.

He pulled away from her a little and ground her nipple lightly between his teeth. Again Ophelia moaned. She let go of his balls and cuppled the back of his head, tangling her fingers in his black hair and groaning as she pressed him tighter against her breast.

"I'd do anything for you, Skye," Ophelia whispered.

Fargo began to think there was something not quite believable about Ophelia when he suddenly shuddered as she ran her hands over him, letting one fingernail drag lightly across the exquisitely sensitive skin between his balls and his ass. He couldn't think about anything when she did that.

"Anything, Skye," she whispered again. "Any desire you have. Everything you have ever wanted to do."

She emphasized her willingness by shifting lower under the covers until she could, with a greedy, slurping sound, take him deep into her mouth, until she had impaled her fine throat on his pulsing shaft.

She took all of him that she could, then braced herself on hands and knees over him and pushed down still farther, driving herself onto him until her lips were clamped around the base of his cock and he could feel the tip of her nose nuzzling his balls.

She pulled away from him then and laughed. Turning her face to him, she gave him a wink, then provocatively licked her lips with the tip of her pink, wet tongue. She gave him a catlike smile, then once again lowered her head and began to suck him.

When he finally came, Fargo thought his toenails were going to be pulled along on the flow that poured into her throat. The release was incredibly powerful and complete.

Ophelia stayed with him, still sucking, until the last drop had been expended. And then she used her fingers to try to milk more of the hot, sticky fluid onto her lips.

"So good," she mumbled. "So nice."

Fargo could not disagree.

Hell, at that moment he couldn't have disagreed with her about anything. He stroked her back and rubbed lightly at the back of her neck. Maybe his luck was changing. He wouldn't mind spending a few more nights with this lady, not at all.

Fargo woke with the dawning of a bright and beautiful morning, the sky blue and almost cloudless for the first time in days. He hadn't intended to stay here through the night. He had wanted to let the horses and people rest for a matter of hours, then move them down the trail on the east side of the pass through the remainder of the night. Instead, his resources drained by the persistent Ophelia, he and all the others had slept on through until daybreak.

Ophelia wasn't at his side. He spotted her a few feet

away, on the other side of the clear space beneath the spruce clump, pulling on her skirts.

Fargo reached down inside the bedroll and retrieved his clothes. He began to pull them on without leaving the protection of the sougan. The morning was exceptionally cold. He stamped into his boots—they were damned cold after being left outside the bedroll during the night—and stretched. He yawned and looked down the cold, empty trail, back toward the San Luis Valley.

"Seems those boys that were following us have given up," he said.

"How can you be so sure?"

"Two things. One, they've had more than enough time to catch up if that's what they were planning." He grinned and added. "The other thing is even surer. If you're going to get caught, it's going to be at the worst possible time. And last night when I was fool enough to fall sound asleep would've been the worst possible time for them to come. They didn't come then, so I got to figure they aren't coming at all."

Ophelia smiled brightly. "That is good, isn't it?"

"I would have to say that it is, yes, ma'am." Fargo rolled his sougan and blanket into a tight roll, buckled on his Colt, and picked up the Sharps. "Come on."

He crawled out from under the spruce and stood, yawning again. He must have been tired to sleep so long and so well. It wasn't like him to forget himself like that when there was the possibility of danger about. And although he had thoroughly enjoyed the reason for his complete exhaustion, he now regretted the resulting inattention. It was only dumb luck that had let them get away with it.

The cold air was so still that Fargo could hear one of

the other players snapping twigs down below as they got ready to build the fire again. Obviously they had let it go out during the night.

He could hear the dull thud of hooves striking frozen earth as the horses pawed through the snow in search of last year's grasses. The air was completely still but bitterly cold.

Fargo stood where he was for a while, examining everything in sight to make sure no one had broken a new trail in an encircling movment around the sleeping camp. There seemed little danger of that, since the sun was fully up now and any planned dawn raid would already have taken place.

As far as he could see there was nothing out of place. Nothing was moving except the people of his own party and the slow, majestic drift of the clouds overhead.

"Is everything all right?" Ophelia asked.

"Seems like it." He took another long look around. It was like the entire world had been frozen into immobility. The silence and the miles-long stretch of unbroken snow off toward the rising sun were almost ghostly. "You go on down," he said. "Take my gear with you. In the left-hand saddle pocket there's a pot. Melt some snow and get some water boiling. I'll be along directly."

"Did you see . . . ?"

He shook his head. "No. Now do as I tell you."

"All right." She gave him a quick kiss, then floundered away through the deep snow.

Fargo climbed higher, hoping but not really expecting to find some game worth shooting amid the trees.

He found nothing to eat, not so much as a junco to boil into a broth, but he did find some juniper growing in the shade of some massive rocks. He knelt by the twisted bushes and stripped away the hard, dead outer bark, then peeled off a double handful of the inner bark. The smell of it was rich and clean in his nostrils. He carried the bark down to the camp.

Ophelia had the water at a slow boil. He gave her the bark, and she looked at it with suspicion.

Fargo laughed. "No, we're not going to eat it. You can make a tea from it, though, that won't taste half bad and should put some warm in our bellies."

"If you say so."

"May we assume that the worst is behind us, Mr. Fargo?" Porter asked.

"I expect you probably can," Fargo said. "Unless something fresh goes wrong, we should be down on bare grass before nightfall tonight."

Lofton looked skeptically down the snow-filled white road that lay in front of them.

"I know it doesn't look it from here," Fargo said, "but you'll be surprised at how it thins out as we get lower. This side of the mountains never gets it anywhere near as bad as what's already behind us."

"If you say so."

Fargo let them take their time about filling up with hot juniper tea. He drank several cups of the bland beverage himself and felt the better for it. His stomach had been churning and protesting over its emptiness, and the hot tea gave a sense of filling heat even if that impression was a false and short-lived one. For the moment it felt good.

"All right," Fargo said when the sun was already more than an hour high. "Gather up and let's go."

All of the horses were saddled. Fargo said nothing until he saw Lofton pull his cinches tight.

"Leave those loose," he said, "easier on the animal that way."

"But I thought—"

"You won't be riding today," Fargo interrupted. "Maybe tomorrow, if we get to some open grass in time to give the horses some recovery off it."

Lofton gave him a dirty look but didn't protest, not even when Fargo swung into the saddle of his own pinto and led off, the Ovaro lifting its forefeet high to break the crusted snow.

Fargo let the pinto break trail for a while, then he dismounted and walked in front of the horse, using his own tiring legs to force a path through the soft, clinging snow.

The exertion warmed him, and even though the temperature was probably not much above zero, he soon had to open his coat to allow the cold air to wick away the sweat from his ribs. It always struck him as being wholly illogical that a man could sweat in weather like this. But he not only could work up a sweat, he had to be careful and make sure he didn't allow his clothes to become saturated with it. For as soon as a person stopped moving and stopped sweating in extreme cold, the combination of wet clothing and low temperatures could sap the heat from his body and kill him as dead as any bullet.

They lost elevation quickly, the wagon road dropping abruptly away from the pass and widing toward the vast sweep of the plains, which they could now see before them. The grassland of the plains—that Great American Desert, where the experts said no crops could be grown and no livestock raised, even though it supported herds of buffalo that numbered beyond counting—rolled virtually unbroken from the foot of the mountains all the way to the Mississippi River, a thousand miles or more in front of them.

As they moved lower, Fargo began to see tracks in the snow: bird, coyote, rabbit, and a few deer.

Just past noon, Fargo jumped a plump doe from a stand of low cedar. The doe was fast, but his Sharps was faster, and they had fresh meat to gorge on during the midday break.

The snow was no longer as heavy either. It thinned until it lay at a depth of no more than six inches, and neither horses nor people were having difficulty moving through it.

By four o'clock, he guessed, he could see the ragged, uneven line where the snow petered out. Below that point was bare earth and brown, stem-cured grass that would fill the horses' bellies and give them the nourishment they needed. Fargo wondered if the Porter Players had any idea how fortunate they were to come down this side of La Veta with horses and humans all still alive.

They had no idea of it at all, he told himself. But then they didn't need to have. That was what they were paying him for.

"All right," he said as they stumbled down a final incline into a pocket of exposed grass. "Hobble the horses and turn them loose. Get yourselves enough wood for a helluva fire, and get me a bed of good coals ready. I'll be back in an hour or less with fresh meat."

He balanced the Sharps over his pommel and turned the pinto north, toward some distant thickets where he would probably find enough meat to last them for the next week. Behind him the Porter Players' voices were shrill and cheerful as the members of the troupe tried to pretend, now that the crossing was behind them, that each one of them had known all along that there was nothing to be worried about.

The horses were in such poor condition after the short-ration crossing that Fargo had the group lay over for a full day for the benefit of the animals. Down at this elevation, with the snow behind them, Fargo had no trouble finding more than enough meat, and the horses were able to fill up on the dry, stem-curled grasses at the fringe of the plains. The grass looked like nothing better than last year's weeds, and an eastern farmer would have refused to allow his animals to eat it, but countless generations of buffalo and antelope had long since proven its value. There probably was no better feed to be found anywhere.

Nor did the people suffer from want, now that they were out of the snow. Fargo's Sharps brought down a yearling elk calf that, baby though it was, would have outweighed a full-grown Mexican steer. The calf was so large that Fargo had to pack it in to camp by quarters, and so tender that no knife was needed to cut the meat after Ophelia broiled the thick steaks over open coals.

That afternoon, while the hobbled horses grazed contentedly nearby, the Porter Players put on a show for their guide's benefit.

Amon Porter, seeming taller and straighter when he assumed the role as troupe leader, recited a soliloquy from a play Fargo had never heard. Fargo guessed that if he knew what the hell was supposed to be going on, he would really have enjoyed it. As it was he was impressed by the old boy's abilities.

The duo of Elliot Croft and Charles Loften performed next, delivering a comedy routine with such straight-faced sincerity and precise timing that Fargo found himself chuckling aloud even though he'd heard most of the jokes at least twice annually since he was old enough to recognize human speech.

Then Catherine Loy, the ingenue of the outfit, played a damsel in distress opposite Porter's villain. Catherine fluttered her eyes wildly and wrung out her heart with anguish as the dastardly Porter threatened her dear old widowed mother with disgrace and poverty if the sobbing girl did not consent to become his bride.

The players had saved the best for last, with Croft as an eager swain seeking the favors of a cool and regal Ophelia Margot, whose presence was such that she made a travel-soiled cape seem to become ermine and an aspen twig turn into a scepter of gold and jewels.

The Trailsman applauded loudly when the Porter Players lined themselves up before him and formally bowed to their audience of one.

"Bravo. Bravo," he called. They bowed again, then gathered around him.

"As you see, sir," Porter said in a booming, theatrical voice, "our little troupe is not without merit."

"You're damn good," Fargo said, "all of you, and I thank you for the entertainment."

"The pleasure was ours, sir," Porter said with a small bow.

Ophelia, perhaps carried away by the spirit of her performance, extended the back of her hand for Fargo to kiss. He did, laughing as he did so.

Catherine turned her head away with a shy smile. Only Croft and Lofton seemed unaffected by the exhilaration of the performances. They were once again keeping quietly to themselves in the background.

"Mighty nice, folks. Thanks." Fargo turned and went to their makeshift larder, using his knife to slice thick steaks from a haunch of tender elk calf. Ophelia was already busy fussing with the few cooking utensils Fargo carried on the pinto. All the rest of their gear had been lost with the mules back at Fort Garland.

"The only thing that would make this any better," Fargo said, "would be some coffee. But I reckon we can restock at El Pueblo. It isn't all that far. A day, maybe a little more than that to the Arkansas, then downriver to El Pueblo. Got to backtrack a little for that, but we need the supplies."

Porter looked alarmed. "We cannot afford to lose time for the sake of a bag of coffee, Mr. Fargo. We have lost entirely too much time already, you see. And speed is essential to our journey. I thought you understood that."

"I know what you told me. But it's not likely anyone will be leaving Leadville for a while. If the valley got that much of a blow, the high country ought to be buried. There won't be anybody leaving there for a spell unless he has to."

"Really, Mr. Fargo, you still fail to comprehend our urgency. We must be there at the very earliest opportunity."

Fargo shook his head.

"I insist, sir. We simply cannot afford the time for diversionary side trips to this El Whatever place."

"Look, Porter, I know you're footing the bill here,

but we need coffee and salt at the least, a helluva lot more than that if you want the comforts you folks all seem to enjoy. And those horses still need grain. There's no forage worth a damn up along the Arkansas. Maybe you've never been up that gorge, but it's solid rock on both sides. Nothing for an animal to eat for miles and miles.''

"Isn't there another access?'' Porter asked. "I believe I heard of another, easier route through the mountains with grass and water in excellent quantity."

"Yeah, there's another way. There's a pass just north of Pikes Peak, then out across the Bayou Salado, up by Tarryall and Bailey and those camps. But I thought you said you were in a hurry. That way would be a day, maybe day and a half, longer."

Porter looked at him with a condescending smile. "And how long would this side excursion require?''

Fargo shrugged. "A day each way, I'd figure.''

"Two days total, then. As opposed to a day or day and a half via the Bayou Salado route.''

Fargo sighed. How do you make a city man comprehend the importance of grain to a horse in winter?

Still, Porter was the man who was paying the bills. And this time Fargo couldn't honestly say that one route was safer than the other. If Porter insisted on bypassing El Pueblo, they could still resupply at Fountain, up near the foot of the pass that would lead to the Bayou Salado.

Come to think of it maybe the man was right, after all. Maybe the Bayou Salado route would wind up being the quicker. Fargo had never been to Fountain, but he had heard of it.

"All right,'' he said.

Porter beamed. "Excellent. Thank you."

Fargo shrugged.

"Amon. Skye. Your steaks are ready," Ophelia called to them.

Fargo grunted as he pulled off the second boot and set it aside. He arranged the Colt and the Sharps where he wanted them and slipped under the thick sougan. As usual, he had laid his bedroll well apart from the rest of them.

That was another thing, he reminded himself. When they reached Fountain, they would have to buy bedding to replace the things that had been lost on the other side of La Veta. Probably the group was tired of sleeping under horse blankets. For sure Fargo was becoming tired of smelling them afterward.

He lay back, his fingers laced behind his head, listening to the Porter Players singing around the fire. They seemed to be enjoying their day of rest in spite of Porter's protests about the need for speed.

The men concluded a song, all three male voices blending into a fine, deep tone, and Ophelia picked up with another number. Apparently it'd be some time before she left the group. Fargo was thinking perhaps he should try to get a little sleep now while he could. With both of them so well rested today, it could well turn into a long and vigorous night ahead. That thought didn't displease him.

There was a sound in the grass to Fargo's right. The noise was made by something too heavy to be a mouse or rabbit, and it came from too close to his bed to be a mule or an elk. He didn't change position, but one hand dropped away to the butt of the Colt.

"Fargo." The voice was a whisper.

"Catherine?" He was surprised. He had scarcely spoken to her since that first night. It seemed a long time ago.

Fargo held the edge of the sougan up so she could come under it with him. She wasn't wearing her cape. She had her arms wrapped around herself and was shivering. She lay down beside him, and he wrapped his arms around her. Her eyes were very large.

"I know what'll warm you up," Fargo whispered. He kissed her.

Catherine was stiff at first. But, she melted quickly, her body shifting to accommodate his and her mouth opening under his firm kiss. She squeezed her eyes shut and began to moan softly.

Fargo's head roved over the cloth of her dress, touching her breast, then down across the flat of her stomach. She parted her thighs as he tugged at the cloth, drawing the hem of the dress up until he could reach under it. She wasn't wearing any undergarments, as he quickly discovered.

"Not so cold there," he whispered.

"We need to talk."

"Yeah," he agreed. "Later."

"Oh, Fargo, I—"

He kissed her again. When he did so, his hand touched and probed. She was wet and receptive, and her breath was becoming shallow and rapid.

Eagerly she reached for him, fumbling with his buckle and the buttons of his fly.

"Hurry," she said breathlessly.

He raised himself over her and held himself there for a moment while she found and guided him.

When he entered her, she was searingly hot. Her hips began to move in the ancient, insistent pattern almost at once.

She raised her legs, locking her ankles behind him. Her arms wrapped tight around him.

Fargo entered her deeply, enjoying the feel of her flesh around his shaft, then slowly began to stroke in and out with long, deep penetrations.

He could feel her rising pleasure in the clench of her thighs, the stiffening of her back, the rhythm of her breathing.

"Hurry," she said again.

Fargo wanted it to last, though, and continued his slow stroking.

Catherine whimpered and bit at his neck. Her hips began to pulse and gyrate, rising to meet him so that she was impaling herself on his manhood.

She came the first time long before he was ready, arching her back and trying to muffle a glad cry in the hollow of his throat. He could feel the convulsive clutch of her sex tight around his shaft.

Catherine went limp beneath him for a moment. Then her eyes went wide as she realized that he hadn't varied his strokes. He was still there, still hard, still unhurriedly moving in and out of her body. Fargo smiled at her and bent his head to kiss her.

"Oh, Skye." She began to move again, with him this time, and he could feel the return of her pleasure as his became more and more insistent.

He knew she was ready again. He could feel the joyous tensions in her body. He began to pump into her harder and faster, driving himself into her, and Catherine responded gladly. "Yes," she whispered.

Yes indeed, he thought. The dam burst, hot seed gushing into her. He held himself rigid, enjoying the flow of it. He was dimly aware that she had crossed that same threshold. She was shuddering and gasping beneath him, clutching him to her with arms and legs and lips, willing herself not to cry out loud.

Fargo relaxed and let his weight down onto her, enjoying the feel of her under him, drained and satisfied for the moment, at least.

7

Catherine murmured with pleasure as Fargo ran his hands over her smooth skin. Her arms snaked around him, and she kissed him.

Fargo was still inside her. He began to get hard again. Catherine felt the change and sighed happily.

Then her expression became serious and she pulled her lips away from his. "Skye, please. I have to talk to you."

"Later."

"That's what you said before."

He grinned. "But later hasn't got here yet."

"Seriously. I do have to talk to you. But only for a minute."

"If you insist."

The girl looked suddenly shy again. She turned her face away from his. Fargo found the change disconcerting, especially since his cock was still socketed within her body, both of them still coated by the juices he had just a few minutes before spilled into her.

"It's about Amon. And the rest of the troupe."

"Yes?"

"I don't think you know—"

"Well, what have we here? The little ingenue grown

up? Do you believe you are ready for leading roles, my dear?'' The voice was Ophelia's. Fargo twisted, in the saddle as it were, and saw her standing over them. He hadn't even heard her approach; his concentration had been elsewhere. He could feel his erection fading, even though Ophelia Margot damn sure had no claim on him. It was just that the idea of being watched wasn't his notion of good fun and games.

Catherine yelped softly and began to blush a furious red. She pushed Fargo off of her and reached under the covers to shove her dress down over her hips.

Ophelia began to laugh.

"That wasn't very nice of you," Fargo told the older woman.

"Humph! It wasn't very nice of her to sneak off like that either," Ophelia said. "I told her to stay away from you."

Fargo half-expected some assertion of independence from Catherine, but there was none. Instead the girl scrambled out from under the sougan. She got to her feet and turned helplessly toward Fargo. Her mouth opened, hung like that for a moment, and then closed again. Still blushing, she turned and ran away toward the campfire.

"I'll be damned," Fargo said.

"So shall we all," Ophelia responded, her voice carrying an undertone of satisfaction as her rival disappeared into the night.

Ophelia stretched, then lazily took her time about kicking off her boots and dropping her cape and dress to the ground beside Fargo's bedding. Without waiting for an invitation, she got down and slid under the covers beside Fargo. She was naked and lush. Her skin was chill to his touch after standing unclothed in the cold air, but her body quickly became warm against his.

Fargo felt himself grow hard again as she ran her fingers over his body. He didn't feel quite right about it, but Fargo was never one to pass up a good time.

"What the hell do you mean, you're going to wait here?" Fargo asked. The village of Fountain was in sight, the smoke from its chimneys rising above the cottonwoods that lined the creek of the same name. And now Porter was telling him that the acting troupe intended to wait here while Fargo went in alone to buy the things they needed.

"I have tried to explain to you, Mr. Fargo, how very difficult it is for a group like ours to hurry through any town where our admirers might be located. We are in a hurry, you know, and invariably there are delays when our players appear in public." The man smiled. "Besides, we never want to risk the displeasure of a fan and potential customer. Some of them become quite upset if we cannot take the time to listen to their praises."

"Bullshit," Fargo said.

Porter drew himself stiffly upright. "How dare you, sir. You have not had these experiences. We have had to learn to deal with them."

"It damn sure doesn't make sense to me, Porter."

"Trust us on this matter, Mr. Fargo."

Ophelia kneed her horse close to Fargo's pinto and placed a gloved hand on his wrist. "Amon is telling you the truth, dear. It must be hard for you to understand, but it is the truth."

"I shall give you funds enough to cover any purchases," Porter said. He reached inside his coat and drew out a fat wallet. He removed his gloves, then counted off a sheaf of large-denomination bills.

"That's more than a horse or mule and a load of supplies could cost," Fargo said.

"Yes, but we owe you for more than the days we originally agreed to," Porter said. "Spend what you need and pocket the rest, sir, until the final accounting in Leadville."

Fargo shook his head as he took the money. Damn, but this was a strange crowd. He began to wonder just what Catherine had wanted to tell him about them.

They did have money, though. Porter must have handed him more than three hundred dollars without hardly making a dent in his wad. Fargo had never realized that the acting business could pay so damn well.

"Okay," he said finally. "If that's the way you want it. Are all of you staying here?"

He glanced around. Porter and Ophelia had already indicated that they wouldn't be comfortable going into the town. Croft and Lofton were, as usual, ignoring him. That left only Catherine who might want to ride along with him. But she lowered her eyes and turned her head shyly away.

Fargo shrugged and stuffed the bills into his pocket. "I'll be back by dark or a little after," he said.

"One other thing," Porter cautioned.

"Yeah?"

"It would be doubly embarrassing if the people of this good community discovered that we were here but reluctant to mingle with them. They might think us snobbish, you see. So we would appreciate it if you would not mention that we are nearby."

Fargo nodded and bumped the Ovaro into a high lope along Fountain Creek.

He couldn't understand these theater people—thank goodness he didn't have to—and his suspicions about them were growing. He wished he'd had the chance to talk to Catherine. There was something positively weird going on here.

But he, for one, was going to enjoy a chance to stand inside a heated building with his coat off and a glass of whiskey in his hand. And he intended to take the time to do it. If that meant the Porter Players would reach Leadville an hour or two later, well, the hell with it. That's the way it was just going to be.

"I think somebody's following us," Fargo said as they reached a reasonably level stretch of ground. The riders and the single pack horse Fargo had been able to buy in Fountain had spent the better part of the day climbing into the mountains west of the sacred springs where Indians of all the tribes came to worship Manitou. He glanced at the sky toward the west but could no longer see the sun. A heavy line of dirty gray cloud was moving in from that direction, which made him think that they soon might have more to worry about than the possibility that Porter's competitors had found their trail again.

"Are you sure?" Amon Porter asked.

Fargo shook his head. "There's a fair amount of normal travel up this way now, heading over to Leadville the same as we're doing. But somebody's back there. Could be just a party of gold-hunters. Could be something else."

"I don't want to take any chances," Porter said.

Fargo looked down the back trail, then to the west again. "Tell you what," he said after a moment of thought. "It's late enough that it won't hurt to pull it in for the evening anyhow. For sure the horses can use the rest after the climb. There's a canyon that branches off to the south. We can slip in there without those other folks knowing. There's enough tracks on the road to cover it if we're careful where we leave the path. Whoever it is can go on by, and we won't have to worry about them."

"If you think so."

He shrugged. "Like I said, it could be just some people on the road west. No point getting excited about it yet, but no point taking any chances either."

The Trailsman led off, keeping to the public road—once a game trail, later a Ute migratory route, and now a wagon road that had been crudely improved in the worst spots—until he found a place where they could angle off into a snow melt that was cutting into the gravel and clay road surface. No one was likely to spot their tracks there, even if anyone was watching for such a trick.

They crossed a grass flat and splashed through the creek that gave Fountain its name, then rode another three-quarters of a mile into a shaded canyon. The air was cold in the steep-walled canyon, and there were banks of old snow remaining there although most of the recent snow had already melted on the exposed ground along the public road.

"This should do," Fargo said. He pointed to a small shelf of gravel that lay above a narrow tributary creek that through the passage of ages had carved the canyon.

"It's lovely," Ophelia Margot said.

Fargo grunted his agreement. He hadn't thought about it, but the spot was attractive. The site was walled with thick patches of mountain willow, and tall pines grew on the slopes to either side. The creek, running full from the melting snow, gave off a low, merry chuckle.

"Go ahead and lay the fire but don't light it yet," Fargo instructed as Croft and Lofton began the work of setting up camp. "No sense in showing any smoke back here. Just in case. We'll start the fire after dark."

The players went about the camp chores efficiently, almost back to normal despite the loss of their gear back in the San Luis. Fargo hadn't been able to find any tents at a fair price in Fountain but had bought some blankets and a pair of tarps that they could rig as lean-to shelters. As always, the first things the senior members of the troupe took care of were their precious script case and makeup bag. They hadn't been left with the mules, that's for sure, Fargo grunted to himself.

Fargo left them to their work and laid out his own bed well away from the others.

Sometime during the night Fargo woke to the sting of snowflakes on his face. He scowled as he shook awake Ophelia and sent her back to the lean-to. Then he pulled his sougan over his head and went back to sleep. When he woke again, shortly before dawn, there was a full-blown storm raging.

"Might be best," Fargo said when the others were up and about, "to hole up here until this thing blows over."

"It doesn't seem all that bad," Porter said.

"We're out of the wind here. All we're getting under that wall of rock up there is the snow and a bit of eddying. Out on the road, though, there won't be any protection from it. And we'd be going straight into the teeth of the thing. Nobody sensible is going to be out in this," he said.

Porter smiled. "Then if those men you saw yesterday were sent by our, uh, competitor, they should be sheltered somewhere?"

"If they got any sense they will be."

"All the more reason for us to press on, sir," Porter said. "Besides which, we cannot afford any more delay. It would be worth a great deal to me, Fargo. A bonus above your daily rate of pay. Say, two hundred dollars additional."

Fargo looked down the canyon. The wind would be hell out there on the road, and the snow was falling heavily. The first storm mustn't have been quite so bad up here as it had been back in the San Luis, but this one looked as if it were making up for it.

"I don't like it, but I can get you through," Fargo admitted.

Porter nodded with satisfaction and got his people busy breaking camp.

"Better have a hot, heavy meal before we pull out then," Fargo said. "You'll need it."

He was hoping that the storm would be a brief one, that it would slack off soon. Instead, it was blowing even harder by the time they left the canyon and broke through new drifts to reach the road.

There were damn sure no tracks on the road now, only unbroken white where the road surface lay hidden. Fargo bundled himself deep into the collar of his coat and turned in the saddle to look at the line of horses that followed obediently behind his pinto. Porter and all of his people were huddled into their clothing, their faces covered as well as possible. They had to be miserable. Fargo was.

The wind was coming out of the west. The road led straight into it. Into the wind and into the sharp bite of the driving snow. Already Fargo could feel the driven snow crusting on his eyebrows and lashes. He ducked his chin low and moved out. Crazy bunch of bastards, he thought glumly as he rode.

Twice during the morning he had to stop and dismount to use his gloved hands to wipe the horses' eyes and muzzles free of caked snow.

"Get off," he yelled above the whip of the wind. "Move around some. Get your blood to stirring."

Catherine did as he directed, and Amon Porter. Ophelia and the two men stayed in their saddles while Fargo and the others stamped in circles through the deep snow and slapped numb hands against their legs.

They nooned in the dubious shelter of a clump of leafless aspen. The protection by the slim white trunks was primarily in the mind. There simply was not enough bulk to the slender trees to give any real respite from the cold cut of the wind.

There was dead wood aplenty for a month of cooking fires, but the wind was too strong to allow a flame to take hold. Lofton and Croft tried for the better part of a half-hour to get a fire started, but all they accomplished was the wasting of several boxes of the matches Fargo had laid in with their supplies.

"Quit trying," Fargo told them. He had to raise his voice almost to a shout to make himself heard, even from a distance of only a few yards. "Walk around, dammit. Get the blood moving."

The two persisted, though, huddled in the snow on their knees while Fargo drove everyone else in small circles to get some flex into their toes. He himself had already switched back to moccasins and was grateful to have them. He probably was the only one in the crowd whose feet were reasonably comfortable.

After a scanty meal of jerked beef—anything with moisture in it would have been frozen too solid to chew—he made them return to their saddles.

Amon Porter, shivering and pale, took Fargo by the elbow and shook his head. The Trailsman doubted that he'd ever seen a more miserable-looking human being than the old actor.

"I think I made a mistake this morning," Porter said. "I think we should stop for the day now."

Fargo explained patiently. "You wouldn't listen to me this morning when we had a place to hide from this storm. Now we have no choice about it. We have no tents and no way to build a safe shelter. If we stop out here in the open, there won't be half of your people left alive, come tomorrow morning. You're in it now until we get out of this damn wind. We got six, maybe eight miles more of open ground. Then the road drops down into another canyon. We have to keep going until we get to some rocks that'll break the wind."

Porter looked like he wanted to cry. But he turned away and climbed laboriously into his saddle. Everyone else was already mounted.

Fargo, as uncomfortable as the rest of them, took up the reins of the Ovaro and pointed the horse once again into the unrelenting snow and wind.

*　　*　　*

They were still far from comfortable, but they were warmer now than they had been since they left the shelter of the canyon and rode out into the face of the storm.

Fargo had forced them past the first branching gullies that led into this water-cut gorge, past that first shelter into the better protection of a sharp rock wall that shielded them now from the worst of the wind.

Unfortunately, this canyon fell in a generally east-to-west direction, allowing the wind and snow to be driven up its length in wild, whistling swirls. The cold was extreme and the drifts were enormous, but this was the best they would be able to do for many miles and many hours of travel. Fargo found the best spot he could and led them to it, the Ovaro having to plunge chest-deep across a massive drift in order to reach a spot out of the direct force of the wind.

"This will have to do," Fargo said. He dismounted, stripped his gear from the pinto, and turned the horse loose to fend for itself through the coming night. None of the animals was likely to go anywhere unless they were forced to it. They, too, would appreciate the shelter from the bitter wind.

The spot he had chosen was at the base of a towering rock wall. A narrow gully led toward the north, sloping sharply upward from the campsite. Below them, out in the twisted but relatively flat floor of the gorge, there was a creek. The year-round run of dark water was buried under a solid bridge of snow now, but Fargo remembered it from the last time he had passed this way. It was choked with ancient beaver dams and old lodges. He had seen then very little sign of fresh beaver activity. The mountain streams had been trapped out years before, back when the only white men in this country were the free trappers of the fur companies and a very few traders, and the beaver were only beginning to repopulate the once-teeming creeks and rivers.

"There should be some aspen up toward the head of the gully," Fargo told Lofton and Croft. "I want you to cut some saplings—thin stuff, not more than two or three inches through—and bring them back here, then all the dead wood you can find. We'll need some for the fire, of course, and the green saplings to make a shelter. Gonna have to put both tarps together and all sleep in a heap tonight. You boys go ahead and do that. I'll take care of the horses. They all need a good rubdown and drying off, and I want to see that it's done right."

He motioned to the women and said, "You two can begin clearing off a space over there against the rock. There's nothing to use for a heat reflector here, so tonight we'll build our fire inside the lean-to we're going to make with those tarps. All right?"

Ophelia nodded and set to work. Catherine averted her eyes but did as she was told. She hadn't spoken to him—or for that matter hadn't really looked at him—since the night Ophelia found her in Fargo's bedroll.

One by one Fargo took care of the horses, unsaddling them one at a time and using their blankets to dry the sweat from their backs where they had been protected from the snow all day long. Bitter cold, snow, and wet backs simply don't mix, Fargo said to himself.

He used his knife to clean the ice from the frogs of their feet and made sure their nostrils were free of ice and snow before he turned them loose. When he was done with one, he moved on to another.

Amon Porter took charge of their supplies and had

things laid out and ready by the time Croft and Lofton were back with the green sapling poles. Fargo had to help them construct the shelter he wanted, using the saplings as braces to place the tarps against the rock wall in lean-to fashion, the high end against the solid stone and the foot banked with piled snow. The only openings were at either end of the crude structure. If they had had blankets to spare, he'd have closed those as well, but that wasn't possible.

"Damn," Fargo muttered as he watched the two actors come back down the gully with loads of light, dry aspen for the fire. "Croft, come over here."

The man dropped his armload of dead wood beside the newly constructed lean-to and walked over to where Fargo was cleaning the feet of the last of the horses.

Croft walked with an odd motion, lifting his knees unnaturally high and placing his boots down with a jerky snap at every footfall.

"You're walking funny. Anything wrong with your feet?" Fargo asked.

Croft shook his head. "Nothing now, thanks. They were awfully cold earlier, but they're fine now."

Fargo groaned and took the man by the elbow, leading him toward the lean-to. Smoke was drifting out of the north end of the shelter, so the women had the fire started.

"What are you doing?" Croft asked.

"Taking a look at your feet." Fargo pushed him down into the lean-to and seated him on the piled bedding near the fire. "Damn you, Croft, you should've exercised today the way I told you to."

"But my feet are fine. Truly."

"Yeah," Fargo muttered. "I'll just bet they are."

He knelt in front of the man and pulled Croft's boots off. "Turn your head away."

Croft gave Fargo a look that said he thought the Trailsman was suddenly daft, but he humored Fargo by looking up the slope toward Lofton, who was laboring up the gully for another load of firewood.

Already certain of what was going to happen, Fargo took Croft's big toe between his thumb and forefinger and squeezed down on it as hard as he could.

The pinch should have been excruciating. But Croft didn't react at all.

"That didn't hurt?"

"What didn't hurt?"

"Shit," Fargo muttered.

Porter and the two women moved close to see what Fargo was doing. They were all on hands and knees. There was no room inside the lean-to to stand.

"What is it, Fargo?" Porter asked.

By the way of an answer, Fargo stripped Croft's soiled sock off the man's foot, exposing skin that was a pale, sickly white from the toes back nearly to the instep.

He pinched Croft's toes again, this time with the man watching. Croft's eyes went wide and he began to whimper. "Oh, my God. I didn't feel that. I . . . you were fooling me, weren't you?"

Fargo didn't bother to answer.

"Frostbite?" Ophelia asked.

Fargo sighed. "Yeah."

Croft, openly weeping now, twisted away from Fargo and shoved his feet toward the warmth of the crackling fire.

"Don't do that," Fargo exclaimed.

"But I have to get them warm, don't I?"

"Not like that. You got them good and frozen. You can't change that now. Stick them by the fire and you'll just make it worse."

"I don't understand."

Just to make sure the damage was as bad as it looked, Fargo took a sharp twig and poked it into the ball of Croft's foot. The man didn't react at all. There was no feeling that far back, and the flesh didn't yield the way it should have. At least half of his foot was frozen.

"You aren't going to like this," Fargo said, "but there's no other way to tell you. This foot, and probably the other one too, are going to have to come off."

Croft sagged back against the frozen rock wall behind him and began to blubber.

"I can't do it," Fargo added. "You'll need a regular doctor for that. We'll get you to one as quick as we can. Meantime, you don't dare thaw it out now that it's frozen."

"But surely—" Porter began.

Fargo shook his head. "There's no help for it. We'll get him down to a doctor, as fast as we can. Meantime, though, he can't get his feet anywhere near a fire; it would only make it worse. Gangrene is bad from frostbite, and it comes on in a hurry. Put those feet over near a fire and thaw them out fast, and he likely won't live to get to a doctor." Fargo rubbed the back of his neck. "Hell, I'm no doctor, and maybe the sawbones will have some newfangled way to save his feet. But I know damn good and well he's a dead man if he puts his feet near that fire. I've seen it happen before."

Fargo had been talking to Porter and the two women. Elliot Croft had withdrawn into a private place of fear and misery. Fargo doubted that the man had heard or understood two words that Fargo had said.

"We'll do what we can for him," Fargo said. "Meantime, I want to check the rest of you too."

He inspected their toes, but none of them was in bad shape. Charles Lofton, when he returned to the shelter with another load of wood, proved to have a very minor case of frostbite, but the freezing wasn't bad and was confined to the tips of his toes.

"Set there on the blankets for a bit," Fargo told him, "and rub your toes with your hands. You'll be all right."

Fargo shook his head. He wondered why Croft was in such bad condition when he and Lofton had done virtually the same things all day long. But then Croft was older. Probably his circulation wasn't as good as the younger man's.

The two men were side by side on the blankets, holding on to each other, both of them bawling like a pair of grade-school kids. Sobbing and sniffling, they were rubbing each other's feet.

The women were upset too, and Catherine was doing some crying right along with the two men.

The only ones who seemed unaffected by the news about Croft were Ophelia and—funny thing about that—Amon Porter. Porter seemed to be taking pretty well that he would probably lose the services of his leading man just when the outfit was about to get their big break, Fargo thought grimly.

The Trailsman shook his head again. As much time as he had spent with this crowd, he still couldn't figure them out. But he was definitely getting more and more suspicious with each passing day. They were up to something, but he just couldn't figure it out.

He gave up trying and left the lean-to. It looked like, if anyone was going to finish the job of hauling in firewood for the night, he was going to have to be the one to do it.

The wind and the snow stopped during the night as abruptly as if some unseen hand had closed a door on them. The sudden end of the wind roar woke Fargo. He raised up a little, careful not to disturb the others who slept beside him in the crude shelter, and smelled the quiet air. The cold was intense. It was probably just as well that he had no idea just how bad it was.

By morning, though, the temperature had risen to something well above zero, and there was once again snow falling. The flakes were large and fluffy. Fargo supposed it could be considered an improvement, for the temperature wasn't bad and this time there was no wind to pile the drifts even deeper than they already were.

He left the bed he had shared with the Porter Players and duck-walked over the legs of the sleeping players until he reached the ashes of last night's fire. He dug into them with a thin stick until he reached the live coals that had been buried under the protective layer of ash, and laid the stick over them. The dry wood smoldered and then burst into flame, and he quickly added more. They were going to need another hot breakfast; the nearest shelter was miles away.

The best thing to do, he thought, would be to turn back the way they had come. There likely would be a doctor for Croft at Colorado City, which was a few miles nearer than Fountain. Either was closer than Leadville.

Behind him he could sense the stirring and groaning of people coming awake as the smoke from the new fire stung their nostrils.

"Good morning," Ophelia whispered. "Or is it?"

"Not as bad as it might've been." Fargo added some more wood to the fire, and the blaze began to spread warmth through the lean-to.

One by one the others pulled the mass of piled blankets down from their faces and blinked their way into the new day. Even Elliot Croft appeared normal. Until he remembered the horror that was still happening to him. Then his face twisted and he began to cry again. Lofton lay at his side, offering the comfort of frequent pats on his shoulder and low, whispered words that Fargo couldn't hear.

Croft seemed to relax a little under his friend's attentions. After a few minutes he even sat up.

"You ladies better see to some cooking," Fargo said. "I'll go out and check the horses." He pulled on his gauntlets and crawled out of the shelter.

The horses were huddled together not fifty yards from the lean-to, their broad backs crusty with layers of ice and snow. Frost rimmed their muzzles and was coated thick on their whiskers, giving them a comical appearance. The Ovaro whickered softly when Fargo came into view and turned to meet him.

"Hang in there, old boy," Fargo said softly to the horse. "We'll get you some grain here." He bent to the sack he had purchased in Fountain.

Behind him he heard a short, squealing scream. And then another.

He turned in time to see Elliot Croft come stumbling out from under the shelter of the tarp, legs wobbly and his feet bare in the deep snow.

"It hurts. Oh, God, it hurts." Croft was dancing on his frozen feet, his legs jittering and pumping.

Fargo realized what was happening. During the night under the blankets with the shared warmth of all their bodies, Croft's feet had begun to thaw. Not much, probably, but enough that now some blood was beginning to move through portions of the damaged appendages. The feeling would have been the same pins-and-needles sensation of a "sleeping" arm returning to use but magnified a thousandfold. The pain would be agonizing.

"Get back inside," Fargo yelled at him.

Croft either didn't hear or ignored him. Instead, the man panicked and began to run barefoot through the snow, away from the lean-to and the horses and down toward the snow-clogged road.

Fargo started after him, then saw that Lofton had come bolting outside and was running after his friend. Croft was barefoot. But then he had already done nearly all the damage he could do to himself. But Lofton was running after him in his stockinged feet. Apparently he hadn't taken time to pull on his boots before he chased after his pal.

Resigned to the stupidity of tenderfeet—it was an expression that was taking on new meaning this trip— Fargo began to trudge after them.

Croft ran at a furious, stumbling pace down onto the road and across it.

"Look out!" Fargo's shouted warning was too late.

Croft fled across the roadbed and out onto the deceptive flat that lay beyond it.

One moment the man was running, the next he was gone from view.

"Stop, Lofton," Fargo yelled. "Don't follow him out there."

The advice wasn't taken. Lofton rushed headlong after his friend. Fargo heard him yelp once as he reached the bank of the creek that lay hidden under the snow. Lofton tried to stop, waving his arms in the air in an attempt to gain balance. Then he too dropped through the soft snow.

This time enough of the blanketing snow had been beaten down for the sound of a splash to reach Fargo's ears. Both had gone into the near-freezing water.

Fargo ran toward them. They'd be wet to the waist, or worse.

Damn fools, Fargo grumbled as he ran. Both of them would have to strip off all their clothes to be dried at the fire. That would take hours, and they needed to get on the road as quickly as possible if they wanted to hold the damage to Croft at nothing more than the loss of his feet.

Still grumbling, Skye Fargo followed the path the two men had broken in the fresh snow. Somehow they had wallowed through a drift that was at least five feet deep between the gully and the flat of the road. Fargo slowed and began to pick his way through the drift in the path they had already broken.

He was not yet out of the drift when he heard the flat, hollow bark of a rifle shot, the sound partially muffled by the sound-absorbent layer of snow on the ground.

Lofton had just crawled back into sight on the bank of the hidden creek, dragging Croft with him.

A moment after Fargo heard the gunshot, Lofton dropped Croft and stood, an expression of confusion crossing his handsome face. He held up a hand and looked at it. It was smeared with bright red.

Lofton turned to look up the canyon toward the flat that they had fought their way across the afternoon before. He still looked puzzled.

Then his body jerked and he threw his arms out wide from his body. He tottered for a moment on his tiptoes and pitched headfirst down the embankment into the icy water of the creek.

The Trailsman was already crouched in the trampled path through the snowdrift. His Colt was in his hand, but the Sharps was back at the lean-to. He hadn't thought to carry it with him when he went to tend to the horses.

From where he was he couldn't see who had fired the gunshots.

On the other hand, the ambushers couldn't see him either.

Keeping low and hidden in the deep snow, Fargo scuttled down toward the creek. He grabbed Lofton, who was lying on his back on the snowy embankment. He felt for a pulse, but the actor was obviously dead.

Croft was sprawled in the icy water a few feet away. "Damn," Fargo muttered. He'd have to leave the shelter of the snow-covered embankment to check him. The Trailsman quickly scanned the area from where the shots had been fired. No movement or sound disturbed the scene. He'd have to chance it.

With his Colt at the ready, he leaned out toward the

man. A shot whistled past his head as he grabbed Croft and pulled him into the snow. He returned the shot, then looked down at the man before him. One glance told him the man was dead. There was a deep gash across the man's forehead. He must have hit his head on a rock when he fell into the creek, Fargo figured.

Satisfied that there was nothing he could do for the men, Fargo carefully crawled back up the gully. When he was out of gunshot, he got to his feet and ran back toward the others.

"Both your boys are dead," Fargo explained as he grabbed up the Sharps and fumbled at his coat pocket to make sure he could feel the bulk of the loose cartridges he carried there. "I'm gonna go give those boys something to think about for a while. I'll be doing some shouting back here to you, but don't pay any mind to what I say. You understand that, Porter?"

The old man nodded.

"While I'm down there, you get the saddles on the horses and get ready to haul out of here. And don't listen to a word I say to you. It'll be a false trail."

"We'll be ready to ride in three minutes," Porter said.

"Saddle the pinto, too. And for God's sake, if you don't take anything else, throw that sack of grain on behind one of the animals. We have to have that."

Before Porter could respond, Fargo was headed back toward the mouth of the gully. He had had time to note, though, that even in the midst of an ambush, Ophelia Margot had her makeup bag in her hand, and Amon Porter was clinging to the script case. He aimed to find out just what was damned sacred about those bags—if he lived through this.

Fargo angled to his left, toward a large boulder that would give him protection. He knelt in the snow behind it and used the cold stone for a rest for the barrel of the Sharps as he leaned forward just far enough to permit him to see up toward the flats.

The falling snow limited his vision, but he could make out a number of dark forms moving against the field of white. Four—no, five of them.

The gunmen were on foot, their horses left behind somewhere, and they were moving with slow caution.

Good, Fargo thought.

He sighted on the nearest of the figures and touched off his shot. His aim was deliberately low.

The heavy slug from the accurate Sharps cut the man's left leg out from under him, and he flopped in the snow.

Fargo smiled bitterly to himself. The shot had been exactly the one he wanted to make. If he had killed the man, the others would have left his body behind. This way, with the rifleman wounded but still alive, there was at least the chance that one of the remaining men would stay with the injured one to help him get away. With luck, then, the one shot would take two of them out of the fight when they came on again.

Before Fargo had time to reload the Sharps, the rest of the men were out of sight, hidden in the deep snow. All it took for a man to get out of view was for him to drop flat on the ground. He didn't have to find anything to hide behind.

Keeping an eye on the area where he had seen the men, Fargo shouted—for their benefit and not for the players—loud and clear. "That's right. Up there in those rocks. And you, over there. They got us bottled up, but by damn we can fort up and give them a hell of a tussle.''

He cocked the Sharps and took aim just below a point where one of the men had recently been standing. Snow was fine for hiding in, but it didn't do a hell of a lot when it came to stopping bullets.

He touched off the shot in what he hoped was more or less the right direction. He heard nothing. But that didn't prove anything. He might or might not have hit someone.

And at the moment he didn't particularly care. Right now he only wanted them to be touchy about the possibilities of being shot from ambush when they decided to move in again.

''That's it,'' Fargo yelled. ''Now stay out of sight until you have a good shot at one. Then blow his fucking head off.''

He smiled thinly to himself. That should give them something to think about.

Fargo turned and eased down away from the boulder. Porter and Catherine already had the horses saddled. As many of them as were needed now, anyway. And Ophelia was busy tying bags and bundles of things behind the cantles.

It was time to slip the hell out of here, up through the other end of the gully, while those riflemen talked things over and convinced themselves they were brave enough to take on what they thought was a forted-up position in a dead-end box.

8

Fargo tied the spare horses to an aspen. The pack horse and the animals Croft and Lofton had ridden were no longer needed for transportation, so they could serve a better purpose now by being left behind. When the riflemen got up their nerve and moved in, it would be helpful if they could see some horses in the camp. For the same reason he stopped Porter when the old man went to take the tarps down from the aspen sapling supports.

"Leave those," he said. "We want those boys to be convinced there's still somebody here. The slower and more careful they are, the better our chances of getting away."

"Do you think we can lose them?" Ophelia asked.

"Not for long," Fargo told her. "With all this snow on the ground, they'll follow us easily once they figure it out. What we're doing now is buying some time, until I can think of something better to do." He mounted the pinto and took them up the gully to the higher ground.

As soon as they gained the higher ground, Fargo turned them west again. There was no point in going back to Fountain now. Elliot Croft was no longer in need of a doctor's services.

Away from the road, which obviously followed the easiest route through the country or it never would have been a game trail and later a public road, the going was rugged.

The terrain rose and fell like a drunk on his way home, and every ridge or fold in the ground meant there was another line of drifts to break.

Even the stouthearted Ovaro was near the end of its endurance before they had gone five miles, and Fargo had no choice but to halt his small group in the protection of some pines so they could give the horses some rest. He loosened the cinches and fed each of the animals a half-gallon of grain.

"At least this snow will slow them as much as it does us," Porter said as he gnawed on a strip of jerky. They hadn't had time for breakfast earlier.

"I wish that was so," Fargo said, "but it isn't. They'll not only be able to follow our tracks wherever we go, but they'll be riding where we've already broken trail for them. Once they start, they'll be able to make a lot better time than us."

Porter began to send worried looks down their back trail after that.

"Are you all right, Catherine?" Fargo asked, moving to the girl's side.

She didn't answer at first, and instead of looking at him when he spoke to her, she first looked at Ophelia Margot, who was standing very close to her. After a moment she turned to Fargo. "It's just . . . Poor Charles, and Elliot. They were a pair of talented dears. I'll miss them."

"Of course you will."

"Do you think they could still be alive? Don't you think they might just have been captured?"

"Captured? Why the hell would a bunch of killers want to take them alive? Even if Croft survived that first bullet, those ambushers would've just finished him when they got the chance."

"But—"

"Catherine." Ophelia's voice was sharp.

The girl ducked her head as if she expected a blow instead of a word. What was she trying to tell him, Fargo wondered. He tried to catch her eye, but she wouldn't look at him again as she walked away to sit beside Amon Porter on a fallen log. The horses made the only noise in the camp with the grinding of their teeth and the shuffling of their feet.

Ophelia sidled over next to Fargo and pressed herself against him. Her hand sought his fly, and the bulge behind it, even though they were in full view of Porter and Catherine. "If we're going to be here a little while," she suggested.

Fargo pushed her away. Just what was the woman up to, he thought. "Good Lord, woman, there could be a bunch of crazy bastards with rifles just behind that last ridge and you're thinking about getting laid?"

"It was just a thought," Ophelia said with a slow smile.

"Forget it," Fargo mumbled. He looked toward Catherine, whose head was turned away. He had to get her alone.

He gave the horses a full hour to eat and rest, regretting every minute of it but knowing the time wasn't wasted. He sat where he could watch along the back trail, a piece of jerky in his hand and the heavy Sharps over his knees. He had no idea how long his ruse would hold the ambushers back along the road.

As soon as he thought it was safe he ordered Porter and the women back onto their horses, then led the way in a sweep back toward the public road. If they could reach that, and if there had been enough traffic along it today to confuse the tracking . . .

It was, he knew, a hell of a lot to hope for.

They rode south, back toward the road, and dropped off the high plateau into a deep, steep-walled gulch that should eventually take them down to the level of the stream and the road.

"Careful here," Fargo warned in a low voice.

Above them the tall, nearly sheer west wall of the gulch, which was almost large enough and deep enough to be considered a canyon in its own right, held a mass of drifted snow that had accumulated during the storm. The still-falling fresh snow was adding to the depth, and high up, near the rim of the gulch, the drifts were wind-torn and corniced, the outer lip of the cornices standing out a good eight or ten feet from the rocky rim of the wall.

"What is it?" Porter asked in a normal tone of voice.

Fargo gave him an angry look and held a finger to his lips. "Shhh. There's two, likely three layers of snow hanging up there, maybe more. We do anything to jar it and it'll avalanche. The snow will fill this floor thirty feet deep and smother anything it doesn't crush. So don't make any noises."

Porter and Ophelia nodded. Catherine looked pale. She began to nervously watch the wall of snow that loomed over their heads.

Fargo rode on slowly, letting the pinto pick its own speed and footing as they made their way past the sheer bank of heavy snow.

Amon Porter and the women might not know much about avalanches, but he'd seen a few of them, a few too many at that. They were more to be avoided than any number of parties of damned ambushers.

And the conditions were right for an avalanche, damn right.

In that drift-prone position, there could be any number of separate layers of snow. And each and every fresh layer made the danger all the more acute.

As one layer of old snow formed a hard crust, it presented a potentially slick surface to the next accumulation of drift. Snow in one solid mass, deposited in a single fall no matter how deep, is unlikely to slide. But each snowfall makes its own deposit layer, building up like so many slabs of separate material.

Any snow left from the earlier storm would form one layer. Then there would be the heavy layer deposited by the more recent storm. And now the continuing snowfall was adding to the weight of the slabs.

And just like two or three flat rocks laid one on top of another and then canted toward the vertical, it was only a matter of time or jarring until one layer of snow might slip across the surface of the next and then the whole damned thing would come roaring down.

And roar it would, if that were to happen. Fargo didn't understand where the sound came from. He had heard someone speculate that it was a wall of air pushed in front of an avalanche that caused all the noise. Whatever the cause, though, they were unbelievably loud. And the force of falling snow was as awesome as that of falling water. Nothing could stand up under it—not roofs, not trees, not even the house-sized boulders that an avalanche could pick up and toss before it like so many matchsticks and pebbles thrown into a raging river.

He looked over his shoulder as they finally cleared the worst and the steepest slope and reached a flatter, wider stretch of ground near the mouth of the gully.

Ahead of them a half-mile or less he could see a flat that was probably the public road.

Fargo spurred the tired pinto toward it.

Then, without warning, he reined the horse to a halt and looked once more behind him, back toward the tall, snow-packed wall on the west side of the gulch.

"Is anything wrong?" Porter asked nervously.

Fargo shook his head. "I just had an idea, that's all. You see that white flat down there?"

Porter nodded.

"I want you to take the women down there. When you get to it, turn off to the right. That's the direction you want. Find yourself a good spot and set up there. You can go ahead and make a fire. And put some coffee on for me. I'll want some when I catch up."

"But where will you be?"

"I'll be watching the back trail for a spell. You folks go along now, and don't forget to loose your cinches. These horses are almost used up."

"All right. If you say so." Porter led on through the unbroken snow, leaving Fargo sitting where he was on the black-and-white Ovaro. Fargo watched them until they were out of sight, so far at least following his instructions, then turned the pinto back up the slope of the gulch.

He pulled the Sharps from its scabbard and dismounted, leaving the pinto in plain sight in the center of the trail.

These boys were really cautious. It was nearly dark before they finally put in an appearance, slipping down along the trail of broken snow with rifles in their hands and with many glances over nervous shoulders to make sure there was no ambush laid on the rims above them.

They were hours behind Fargo's party, and nearly all of that time had been spent back at last night's camp, Fargo figured. His bluff back there had worked better than he'd hoped.

Now he rather regretted that it had worked so well. Because of that he had been hunkered in a pocket of deep—and damn well cold—snow for all the time it had taken the riflemen to catch up with him.

The snow was still falling, but lightly now, and he could see the three figures as soon as they followed the trail to the top of the gulch and started down it.

They came on single-file, saving their horses by staying in the tracks Fargo's pinto had already broken. The animals would be in good shape. Hell, they hadn't traveled but something like seven miles since that morning dust-up when Lofton was tagged. Fargo was glad he didn't have to depend on speed to get Porter and the women away from this bunch.

Fargo was curious about these men. They moved with an almost absurd amount of caution, much slower than Fargo would've gone if he'd been on the other end of this hunt.

Generally speaking, the sort of man who'd put his gun out for hire was a wild, hairy, hell-raising type who just didn't give much of a shit what happened to him, or to anybody else. So Fargo found it interesting and fairly odd that this trio was tracking them so slowly and carefully.

There were only the three of them now, so obviously one had remained with the man Fargo had shot in the leg that morning. That was good; he'd already cut the odds. Now he wanted to finish with these men, get along to Leadville, collect his pay, and find a nice warm spot where he could hole up with a full bottle and a willing woman. The easy money he'd envisioned when Porter asked him to take on the job wasn't turning out to be so damned easy, and Fargo was going to be glad to deliver his outfit to Leadville and be done with them.

Not that there hadn't been certain fringe benefits and all that, but still . . . And what the hell was going on between Catherine and Ophelia? He'd really like to know what Catherine had been trying to tell him.

He thought these things while he waited, crouched low in the snow, as he bided his time to set his plan into action.

He almost felt sorry for the poor bastards who were now a hundred yards deep into the gulch, but not all that sad. Given the clear choice between him and them, the answer was easy.

The leader of the three held up, and the two others stopped behind him, their horses nose to tail in the close confinement of the deep trail.

The man pointed, then turned and said something to his companions.

After a moment all three dismounted, rifles in their hands.

Good, Fargo thought. That was the reason he had

left the Ovaro in plain sight on that white field of snow. It was what he was hoping for.

He looked at the horses and then at the terrain that surrounded them. He really would have been happier if the leader had been a little more alert, if the man had been paying more attention to the open areas in front of him and less to the sheer walls that rose to either side. That way the horses would have been left at the upper end of the gulch and not so far down into it. Still, it looked like the horses might have a chance. Fargo didn't want to destroy any animals if he could avoid it.

He sighed and earred back the knurled hammer of the Sharps.

The three men ducked low but remained in the track that had been beaten into the snow when Fargo and his people came through.

They crouched and moved ahead with their rifles held at the port and with many nervous looks up onto the rims of the gulch.

Fargo let them come. Another hundred yards. Two hundred. He gritted his teeth and forced a patience he didn't feel. He scanned the west rim, high and snow-heavy above them. They were coming under the largest of the cornices now.

Another twenty yards . . . They moved ahead with a slowness that was painful to watch. Five yards, fifteen . . .

Finally.

Fargo shouldered his Sharps and squeezed the shot off almost before the butt plate had time to reach the hollow of his shoulder.

He didn't take careful aim. There was no need.

The heavy bullet was sent hissing somewhere into the mass of the largest of the snow cornices.

In any case, it wasn't the bullet itself that mattered; all he wanted was the noise, the concussive shock of the muzzle report from the big Sharps.

The Trailsman hadn't been wrong about the avalanche potential of that steep wall of heavy snow. The booming report of the Sharps, directed straight at the precariously balanced slabs of snow, did its work.

The shock was enough to start a thin trickle of snow moving on the high slope.

There were only a few flakes at first. Then each of those dislodged others and sent them into motion.

A fist-sized ball of snow fell away from the underlip of the cornice. That spot, weakened from the underside, dropped another wad of packed snow, this one perhaps as large as a man's head.

One small bit sent another into motion, and then another and another.

Slowly at first and then with a gathering rush, the weight of the snow began to shift and slide. And without warning the entire slope directly above the three riflemen was in motion.

There was a low, thrumming hiss of sound in the evening stillness, loud enough to reach Fargo's ears.

One of the men, the one in the middle of the group, looked with horror to his right and shouted something. At least Fargo thought he tried to shout. He could see the man's mouth open, although no sound of the scream reached his ears.

Before that could happen, the faint hiss had turned suddenly into a roar as the thin, trickling initial slide turned into an out-and-out avalanche.

A curling wave of snow ten feet high, shaped very much like an ocean's waves, crashed into a clump of aspen in its path and flooded through the tiny grove, surging with overwhelming force over and around the slender trunks.

Whole trees were mowed down as easily as a stalk of wheat under a sharp scythe. Half of a trunk, its end jagged and splintered, was tossed high into the air, spinning like a stick thrown for a pup to fetch.

The men, trapped beneath the force of the avalanche, tried to run. One of them was still holding on to his rifle. The others had thrown theirs away.

It made no difference, of course, the awesome fury of the avalanche descended too swiftly for any living thing to get out of its way.

With a mighty roar, throwing billowing clouds of powdery snow dozens of yards into the air like a new, low-forming cloud, the avalanche flowed down the slope and over the terrified men.

It flooded the bottom and roared on, racing partway up the opposite wall of the gulch and gathering new snow there to add to its strength before gravity prevailed, and what was left of the white mass curled back onto itself and dropped—as suddenly harmless as it had been suddenly awesome—back onto the floor of the gulch against the east wall.

The west wall now was virtually barren, stripped of snow, vegetation, and topsoil alike by the avalanche.

Fargo stood. He was shivering, even though he wasn't conscious of the cold at all.

The cloud of high-thrown snow settled quickly, leaving behind a white mass that showed here and there the dark thrust of a branch or a broken tree trunk. There was no sign whatsoever of the men. They had disappeared completely.

Fargo shuddered and stamped his numb feet.

Beyond the ugly pile of snow, however, up toward the top of the gulch, he could see two nervous horses tossing their reins and dancing in discomfort. The third horse was on its side but was still alive, partially buried by snow and struggling to get free.

While Fargo watched, the animal got its feet under it and lunged upward, dashing for the comforting security of the presence of its fellows. The horse whinnied and Fargo's Ovaro answered.

The Trailsman turned and began making his way back down to the pinto. He hoped Ophelia had that coffee ready for him. He needed it, or better yet, something stronger.

"In the morning I'll go back for the tarps," Fargo said. His hands were curled around the coffee-warmth coming through the thin metal of the cup Ophelia had handed him. "It's only a few miles back by the road."

A few feet away the horses were munching their evening grain, which was another thing he wanted to get from the camp they had abandoned. They had grabbed only one sack of grain when they left, and Fargo wanted the rest of it. With luck perhaps the pack horse would still be there too.

"Isn't that dangerous?" Ophelia asked. "Might those men not be there?"

Fargo hesitated before he answered. "They won't be there," he said softly.

"Oh."

Amon Porter said nothing, but he looked quite

pleased. "We should be in the clear then, shouldn't we?" he asked after several minutes of silence.

Fargo shrugged. "Leadville's not next door yet. If the road's not too badly drifted, and I don't figure it should be, we'll reach the drop down into the Bayou Salado tomorrow. Then we got to cross it and go either across Mosquito Pass, which should be a son of a bitch after all the snow we've had, or curl back around through Trout Creek Pass and down to the Arkansas River for the last leg up to Leadville. Call it "—he did some swift calculations in his head, trying to anticipate the snow depths and travel conditions—"four days at the least or six at the worst. I know that isn't what you expected, but it's the best we can do."

"I understand," Porter said. The old man seemed unworried about the delay. His impatience for a swift arrival in Leadville seemed to have suddenly disappeared, yet Fargo knew for certain the man had received no outside information from or about that fellow they were supposed to meet there. Did it have something to do with the loss of forty percent of his troupe, Fargo wondered, or the end of those fellows tracking them? Fargo didn't know and truly didn't all that much care. At this point he only wanted to get these people safely delivered and be done with them.

"For tonight," Fargo went on, "since we don't have any other shelter, I'll make us some snow caves. They're warmer than you might think, and Lord knows there's enough material here to build them out of. Then in the morning I'll take a quick trip back to the old camp, pick up the stuff we left there and likely the spare horses, and we'll be off."

"Do you really think the horses will still be there?" Porter asked with apparent interest.

"I don't know it, of course, but I would think so. Them and the grain and the tarps and what food you didn't grab this morning, I think will still be there."

"Excellent." Porter sounded genuinely pleased. Fargo assumed that the man was happy he wouldn't have to sleep in snow caves for the remainder of the trip.

"Well," Fargo said, "I better get to work on those caves so we can get some rest tonight."

He choose to dig the unstable burrows in two separate drifts and quickly scooped out two low-roofed shelters with narrow entries, each of them domed shapes large enough to accommodate three people.

As he had more than half-expected, he hadn't had time to approach sleep before he heard a faint scuffling in the snow outside his cave and then saw Ophelia Margot's attractive head poking through the entrance. She had to get on her hands and knees to get inside the cave. She was carrying a match to light her way.

She blew the match out as soon as she had her bearings, and the cave was plunged into total darkness. Fargo could feel her presence as she crawled to his side.

"Busy darling?"

"I expect to be," he said.

She chuckled as he reached for her and drew her under the sougan beside him.

Her clothes were chill and damp from clinging snow, but that problem was quickly disposed of. She fondled him lightly and then helped him with the buttons of his fly.

"Mmmm," she murmured into his ear as he sprang

free of the restraining cloth, erect and ready. "Lovely."

"How can you tell? It's dark in here."

"I have an excellent memory, dear. And a marvelous imagination."

He took her into his arms and felt her tongue slide warm and wet down the side of his neck, across his throat, and onto the hard, flat planes of his chest.

Fargo positioned himself over her and slid easily and deeply into her. He felt her arms and legs clamp around him, and she raised her hips to him.

"Mmm, yes," she whispered.

Fargo rocked slowly in and out, enjoying the warmth of her. He buried his face in the curls of her hairdo and plunged harder and faster, holding nothing back, until the sweet surge of pleasure rose and rose and finally exploded. His seed gushed into her, filling her beyond capacity and leaking out again to drool down onto his balls. The flow of sticky, cooling fluid tickled.

"Lovely," Ophelia said again, although it was obvious that she had gotten nothing out of it herself.

"If you say so."

"We'll give you a few minutes to rest, dear, and then we shall see what my imagination can do for you."

"I'm just betting you'll be able to think of something, Ophelia."

"And of course you shall be right, dear man," she said with a low chuckle.

And he was.

9

Fargo started the fire and filled the coffeepot with clean snow. The morning was fine, the sky clear for the first time in what seemed like quite a while, and the temperature crisp but not really uncomfortable. He yawned and stretched as Ophelia crawled out of the snow cave they had shared through the night. She had been doing something with her hair when he left; he found it mildly incredible that she was able to keep it as well as she did under the primitive travel conditions.

"Wake up Porter and Catherine," Fargo told her. "You all can get breakfast going while I ride down and fetch back the rest of our things."

"All right." She got down on hands and knees again and crawled halfway into the other cave.

She stopped partway into the short tunnel Fargo had dug and cried out, raising up without first remembering to back out of the tunnel so that snow cascaded over her shoulders, and the entrance to the shelter was destroyed.

"What is it?" Fargo reached her side in a few long strides.

"It's—" Ophelia could not go on.

Fargo pushed her aside and dug his way down into the cave, having to paw a new opening with his hands.

Catherine Loy lay on her side in the low white dome. Her hands and feet had been bound and she had been gagged, a dirty sock stuffed into her mouth and secured in place there with a man's necktie.

There was no sign of Amon Porter.

Fargo crouched at Catherine's side and stripped the gag away from her. A sour stench filled the small cave when he removed the sock from her mouth, and there was yellowish vomit plastered and nearly dry at the back of the wad of cloth.

The girl's skin was cool to the touch.

"Damn," Fargo said.

"What?" Ophelia was still standing at the enlarged and ragged entrance to the cave.

Fargo raised one of the girl's eyelids to make sure, but it was as he'd expected.

"She's dead," he said. "It looks like Porter didn't mean to kill her. He tied her up and left her, but she choked on the gag and tried to spit it up. Likely she choked to death after he was gone."

Ophelia dropped to all fours and crawled into the cave with Fargo and the dead girl.

She paid no attention to Catherine, though, but began quite frantically to search through the jumble of blankets and female clothing that were on the hard-packed floor of the shelter.

"That son of a bitch. Oh, that miserable, lousy son of a *bitch*."

"What're you talking about?" Fargo asked, since the woman was obviously not referring to the demise of Miss Loy.

"The bags, dammit. They're gone."

Fargo glanced around the interior of the small structure. There was no sign of the precious script case or makeup bag. "So?"

Ophelia whirled on him, her eyes flashing with fury. "The bags are gone. He took them. Sent me off with orders to stay the night. Fuck your damned ears off, he told me. Keep you too busy to let you get suspicious, he told me. Then, as soon as my back was turned, the rotten bastard grabbed the bags and took off without me."

Fargo was beginning to understand, and the suspicions that had been swimming in his head finally came into focus. "Money, right?"

Ophelia nodded.

"Currency, I reckon, or you wouldn't have been handling it so easy," he said. Hard money was much more common, but it was also entirely too heavy to carry easily in the quantities that would fit into those cases. "Where'd it come from?"

"What difference does that make?" she snapped.

Fargo grinned at her. "Could make a hell of a difference if I have to decide if I go bring it back or if I just turn you over to the law the next chance I get."

"Oh." Ophelia's eyes went wide, then quickly narrowed. She was thinking swiftly, having only seconds to come up with some suitable lie that would bend the Trailsman to her will.

Fargo sat back and waited calmly. It was rather amusing to watch as she tried to sort out her options.

"It was money from the sale of some stock. Mining shares in Leadville," she said after only a moment's hesitation. "We took it, oh, several years ago in exchange for a debt. No one ever thought it would amount to all that much at the time, but since it wasn't worth anything anyway, we just hung on to it. Then the mine went into bonanza, and the stock was worth a fortune. We sold most of it, you see. That's where all the money came from. And we were going to Leadville to see about the value of the remaining shares. Those men who were chasing us were sent by the man who bought our shares. He wanted the shares and his money back too. And now Amon has run off with all of it. But it's as much mine as it is his, Skye dear. And if you bring it back to me, I'll share it with you. Right down the middle." She smiled. "And you know I'll love to share other things with you too." Her eyelashes were fluttering prettily.

Skye Fargo laughed. It was a genuine, hearty belly-rumbler. "Not bad, Ophelia. Not bad at all, considering you didn't have a script. But what kind of idiot do you think I am? I mean, I knew there was some reason why you were so willing and so accommodating. I had no idea what it was, but I was curious about it. I wanted to see how far you'd take it. But you're good. I got to admit that."

He shook his head. "And I got to admit, too, that you folks did pull one on me. Every time I got suspicious, there you'd be ready and willing to jump in the sack and take my mind off those suspicions. But mining shares? Grow up, honey. *I'm not that dumb*. He reached forward and slapped her across the face. A trickle of blood appeared at the corner of her mouth. "Where did you get all the money?" he repeated.

Ophelia began to cry. Her sobbing was loud and heartrending, her tears wet and quite real.

Fargo sat where he was, unmoved by the performance.

After only a moment Ophelia gave it up, and the tears disappeared as quickly as they had come.

"Where'd you think a pile like that would come from? A bunch of has-beens and never-would-bes like us couldn't get hold of dough like that any way but stealing it. We hit a bank down in Santa Fe when we were there for an engagement." She snorted. "Took in exactly twelve dollars and nineteeen cents over expenses and didn't have enough money in our pokes for transportation to the next shit-heel burg. So I cozied up to this little bald, greasy shit that worked at the bank and got his keys, and the boys took it from there." She shrugged. Then she brightened. "But I'll still share with you, honey, if you find Amon and get those bags back here where they belong." She reached out to fondle his crotch with loving attention.

Fargo laughed again and knocked her hand away. Then a most unwelcome thought occurred to him, and he muttered a few well-selected curses.

"Those weren't competitors or rival thieves that have been after us," he said. "They're the damned law. Posses alerted by telegraph."

Ophelia shrugged an acknowledgment. "Honey, I sure hope you aren't the kind of prissy son of a bitch that would want to turn a girl in for one little mistake."

"What I am," Fargo said, "is the kind of worried son of a bitch that intends to find Amon Porter and get that money back in my hands. *Then* we'll talk about who does what to whom."

Ophelia smiled again. She seemed quite cheerful now. "I knew I could count on you, sweetheart." She sighed.

"Actually, this is working out very nicely. Now there will be just you and me to split the take, honey."

"One thing you got to know, Ophelia. You can pack your twat with snowballs for all I care, but stay the hell away from me. I don't want any knives in my back when I'm having a good time."

"But, honey," Ophelia said, her eyes wide and innocent, "I wouldn't do a thing like that. Not until we have the money back." She barked out a low, throaty laugh, and Fargo felt his skin crawl. This lady was no lady at all.

Fargo's plans to go after Amon Porter were interrupted by the arrival of unexpected guests at the camp.

And these boys were not amateur posse members like the last ones. These boys wore their hides with the fur side out and knew what they were about.

One minute Sky Fargo was busy saddling his pinto, with Ophelia Margot engaged in the production of a breakfast. The next second Fargo was surrounded by men with carbines and rifles and revolvers in their hands and a grim willingness to shoot etched on their faces.

"Easy boys," Fargo said softly. "I'm not about to run." He turned his body so that his side was presented to the nearest of the lawmen and added, "There's a Colt riding under the coat here. We might all feel safer if you were to do me the favor of removing it."

The deputy obliged him.

Fargo nodded. "I have a story to tell you fellows, though I doubt you'll be wanting to believe it after you've heard me through."

"I think we will, Fargo." The voice came from

behind him. Fargo had heard it before but couldn't place it now. Fargo turned.

Sam Bowen, the New Mexico territorial marshal he had met down in Taos, was standing there. Fargo felt one whole hell of a lot better when he saw the marshal's chapped, wind-reddened face and the familiar double-tubed scattergun that dangled loose and relaxed from his left hand.

"I just found out this morning what was going on," Sam," Fargo said. "Wouldn't have known then, I guess, but that damned Porter took off during the night with both bags of cash, and the woman over there got pissed off enough to spill it. There's the other woman lying dead under the snow there, too. But I doubt she was much of a party to the thing."

Bowen nodded. "I know you weren't in on it, Fargo. Hell, I put you onto these people myself before the wire came through. Bastards had cut the line between Santa Fe and Taos, so you were well out of town before I heard."

"I have to tell you something, Sam. I defended these folks some when I thought they were honest. It might've been some of your people that got hurt."

"None of mine, but probably some boys like us." The marshal sighed. "We'll work it out, Fargo. Tom, you can give him his gun back. We got no quarrel with this one."

"How'd you get up to us, Sam? I thought we'd left everybody behind."

Bowen grinned. "Came over Poncha and got ahead of you that way. When we heard on the wire that you'd headed upcountry out of Fountain, me and the boys came on from Fairplay. Started two days ago and been waiting for you."

Fargo whistled. "They said you were hell for getting rid of. I believe it now. Poncha must of been kind of interesting."

"It was for a fact, Fargo. Interesting."

"Do me a favor, Sam?"

"Such as?"

"I'd like to be the one to drag Amon Porter back—him and those two cases of money."

Bowen pursed his lips and thought about it for a moment. "Finish saddling and get mounted. Any idea which way he went?"

"Uh huh."

"Then let's get to it."

Bowen detailed two men to put handcuffs on Ophelia Margot and take her back to Fairplay. Then the rest of the party, including Skye Fargo, rode east, back toward the provisions and the gear the Porter Players had abandoned there the morning before.

"How about that," Fargo mused when they reached the deserted camp. There was no sign of any equipment and no sign of any horses or bodies either. Apparently the wounded deputy and the deputy who was tending him had gathered up everything and used the spare mounts to transport the bodies of Croft and Lofton back toward the plains towns. "Looks like Porter outsmarted himself."

"How's that?" Bowen asked.

Fargo pointed to some tracks in the snow. "The son of a bitch is afoot. He likely didn't want to take the chance of waking me by taking his horse last night, and I'd told him I thought our spares would still be here. So he's somewhere in these rocks without a horse and with two bags full of cash dragging him down.''

"Then we'd best get after him.''

"Is that a braided reata on the side of your saddle, Sam?''

"Yeah.''

"Can you get along without it?''

"I expect I could.''

"It won't be in any fit shape to use again once I'm done with it.''

Bowen shrugged and took down the reata. He tossed it to Fargo.

"You fellows can set up here and take it easy. I'll be back before dark with Porter,'' Fargo said as he dismounted. "I'd appreciate it if you'd keep an eye on my pinto.''

"You're going afoot?''

"If you're chasing a man afoot in this kind of country, you'd best go that way yourself. Too many places a horse can't make it.''

"But the snow will make you as slow as he is, Fargo.''

The Trailsman grinned and shook his head. "Nope.'' He pulled out his knife and used it to cut the ends off Bowen's reata, then plucked the separate strands of rawhide apart until he had half a dozen long, thin strips.

"If you don't have a damn good reason for doing that, Fargo, you owe me the two dollars I paid for it.''

Fargo walked up the slope and cut two thin, supple young aspen saplings from the same stand where Croft and Lofton had gathered the camp wood. The saplings were leafless and dead-looking on the outside, but their pith was still green and limber.

He bent the saplings into oval curves and tied the tails together with strips of Bowen's reata, then began tying on crisscross lacework.

"Snowshoes," Bowen said when he realized what Fargo was doing.

"Uh huh. Walk these things right across the top of the snow where a man without them will be belly-deep and having fits with it."

Bowen grinned at him.

Fargo tied the snowshoes onto his boots and tested them, walking about a little. Bowen, beside him, was thigh-deep in the fluffy snow while Fargo's snowshoes barely sank into the soft surface.

"I'll see you tonight," Fargo said. He left his Sharps with the pinto. The Colt would be enough, especially since he knew for a fact that Porter could not be armed with anything more deadly than a short-range pocket pistol, if that.

Amon Porter was lying, exhausted, at the base of a broad boulder. Fargo knew the man was in trouble long before he reached him. The signs of the snow had been unmistakable where Porter had floundered and fallen with increasing frequency.

Now the old thief was played out and at the end of his rope. Even if he wanted to run, he would not have the strength for it.

Fargo noted with interest that both money satchels were still with the man, though. Porter was lying on his side with one arm wrapped protectively around the loot.

The Trailsman was in no hurry now. He walked across the top of the snow layer, which was more than four feet deep here, as Porter's tracks testified, until he was standing directly over the owner and road manager of the famous Porter Players.

Fargo's shadow passed over Porter's face, getting his attention. His eyes opened.

There was a moment's lag, then they widened in shocked recognition.

"Hello, Porter," Fargo said cheerfully.

"How . . . ?"

"You played me for a fool, Amon. That wasn't a real smart thing for you to do."

"But—"

"Catherine's dead, Amon. You killed her."

"I never."

"Oh, yes you did. She choked to death on that gag you put in her mouth. Pity, too. She was decent. The only one of the crowd that I'd be able to say that about, I think."

"But, I—"

"Point is, Amon, you're wanted now for murder as well as theft. Pretty serious thing, murder."

Porter groaned and blinked, rolling onto his back. He was no longer so worried about his precious hoard of stolen money. Amon Porter was learning that there were things of far greater value than mere money. He looked into Skye Fargo's eyes, and that lesson was driven home like an icy spike plunged deep into his heart.

"You're going to kill me, aren't you?"

"I'm thinking on it, Amon. I surely am. But I'm not the law, Amon, so I'm taking you in."

"Look, Fargo, all this money. Thousands of dollars,

Fargo. Thousands. I'll share it with you," the little man pleaded.

Fargo laughed at him. "If it was the money I was interested in, Amon, I could as easy kill you and then walk away with it. You wouldn't object if I did it that way. And I could have all the money that way too."

"But if it isn't the money . . . ?"

"You used me, Amon. You lied to me and used me and put me in the way of the law. That wasn't a real nice thing for you to do, was it?"

"Here," Porter said. He swept both money cases toward Fargo.

At the same time his other hand crept toward the front of his snow-caked coat.

Porter was probably counting on Fargo to be looking with greed and wonder at the bags that held all that money.

But the Trailsman was watching Amon Porter's hands.

Skye Fargo laughed again. "I wouldn't try anything fancy, Amon. Now get up and start walking."

The old man got slowly to his feet. Pretending to stumble, he went for the pistol in his coat pocket.

"Last mistake, Amon," Fargo said as he grabbed his Colt.

Fargo shot the man in the chest and he fell forward into the snow. A bright-red stain quickly spread through the white.

Fargo looked down at the man lying before him. "Greedy old fool," he murmured not unsympathetically as he holstered the Colt and picked up the two bags full of money. He glanced toward the sky. There was enough daylight remaining, he thought, to make it back to Sam Bowen and his men before full dark. He hoped they had coffee and a hot meal waiting. He could damn sure use both tonight.

LOOKING FORWARD!
The following is the opening section
from the next novel in the exciting
Trailsman series from Signet:

The Trailsman #49

THE SWAMP SLAYERS

*1861, the Louisiana back country,
near the dark and secret places known
as the bayous . . .*

"Now, you're much too pretty a thing to be holding
such a big, ugly gun," Skye Fargo said soothingly. But
it was no quick-talk compliment. The lamp the girl had
set down on the cellar floor showed that she was both
small and pretty, dark-blond hair, an even-featured
face, a nice, small nose, and beautifully formed lips. But
it was her eyes that held him, blue fires that seemed to
burn with a strange light.

"Now, you just put that rifle down and we can talk
nice and proper," Fargo said.

The big, lever-action Volcanic didn't move so much
as a fraction of an inch, he saw. "Throw your gun
down," the girl said.

Fargo hesitated and saw the rifle barrel lift to point directly at his gut. She was too close to miss, and the big Volcanic could blow a buffalo apart at this range. Slowly, he lifted the Colt from its holster and let it slide to the floor. A tremendous bolt of lightning illuminated the cellar with a flash of blue-white light, and the thunderclap shook the house. He saw that the girl had moved a few paces from the stairs that led up to the first floor.

"I told you, I can explain," Fargo said. "I came in to get out of the storm. Christ, you can hear it's something fearful out there. I was lost." The girl said nothing and he went on quickly. "The house seemed deserted. I called out, tried the front door. Nobody answered. I went around and found the storm-cellar entrance."

The burning blue eyes seemed to pierce right through him. She wore an almost-floor length loose shift that hid most of her body under its shapelessness, yet two round, high mounds managed to push into the garment. "Maybe that's the way it was. Maybe not," she said flatly.

"That's just the way it was. I'm telling you the truth," Fargo said.

"Doesn't make any difference," she said almost wearily.

"What do you mean? Of course it makes a difference," Fargo protested.

He saw her shoulders lift in a half-shrug. "You're a dead man either way," she said. She lifted her voice, called out without taking her eyes from him. Or the big rifle, either, he noted. "Igor," she called.

Fargo's eyes went to the top of the stairs as he saw the shadow appear first, then the figure step into view. His frown dug deeper into his brow. The man started down the steps, filling every inch of the stairway, a mountainous figure nearly seven feet tall, Fargo guessed. The giant's shaven head barely cleared the timbers of the roof of the cellar. Small eyes in the heavy face peered at him, a slightly Mongol cast to their shape. The giant wore knee-length, baggy trousers, his chest and arms bare except for a small, embroidered vest that hardly covered the upper part of his torso. Fargo took in a tremendous chest, arms the size of small trees, a belly carrying perhaps ten pounds too much fat. The hulk was awesome, frightening in size and manner as he reached the floor of the cellar of the house and started to lumber forward.

"He's yours, Igor. Enjoy yourself," the girl said.

No small man himself, Fargo felt dwarfed by the hulk and cast a quick glance at the girl. She had stepped back closer to the stairs, but the burning blue eyes looked on excitedly.

"What the hell is this?" Fargo flung at her. "You get your kicks by watching this mountain fall on people?" He peered at her and saw no change in the pretty face as the burning blue eyes continued to watch. He flicked a glance at the Colt on the floor and the huge figure saw the glance, kicked the gun with one foot, and sent it skittering into a corner of the cellar. Fargo moved backward slowly as he let his eyes scan the cellar and take in old brass-fitted trunks, wooden crates, an old bedstand, broken barrels—all the odd and castaway things that find their way into cellars.

He brought his eyes back to the huge figure that lumbered toward him in the dim light of the lamp. Fargo's lips were a thin, tight line as he backed away. None of it had made any damn sense. The girl had just cast aside his explanation. But he hadn't time to wonder about that now. He had to think about staying alive, and he went into a weaving crouch as the huge figure came at him. The giant lifted his huge arms, bulged powerful shoulder muscles, and tried a long, looping left. Fargo dodged it easily, avoided the right that followed, and threw a sharp right cross that landed on the giant's jaw. It was a blow that would have sent most men down, but the huge figure didn't even pause in his lumbering gait.

Fargo ducked another looping blow, drove a whistling uppercut under the man's jaw. This time Igor made a grunting sound as his head snapped back, but he plowed forward again instantly. Fargo moved under another ponderous blow to throw a counter right and saw, in surprise, the tremendous downward blow come at him with a sudden explosion of speed. He tried to turn away, but the blow caught him on the shoulder and felt as though a tree had fallen on him. He fell sideways and stumbled, and another powerful blow caught him in the side. He hit the cellar floor, spun, and regained his feet just in time to avoid a bone-crushing kick. Off balance from the missed kick, the giant figure almost fell forward, and Fargo brought a whistling blow around in a flat arc and drove his fist deep into the giant's kidney.

The blow would have collapsed anyone else and Igor did let out a roar of pain as he spun around. But he came forward again, his little eyes glittering with rage. Fargo feinted, started a hard right, and drew back as he saw the giant's sledgehammer fist poised. The huge man was deceptive, he had learned. His lumbering could explode into astonishing bursts of speed, and Fargo backed from a long left, ducked under another, tried a counterblow, and swung away without delivering it as Igor's huge fist exploded. The swish of air grazed the top of his head as he ducked, pulled away, and watched the brute come at him again.

Igor leapt with a sudden rush and Fargo spun to one side to avoid a treelike arm, and drove a powerful left into the brute's solar plexus. Igor staggered, drew breath in hard, but didn't go down. Fargo brought a hard right up onto the man's jaw, and Igor's head went back. He was wearing the giant down, he told himself, and he stepped in again, his confidence misleading him. The downward blow arced over him with another explosion of speed, and he whirled to avoid it and felt the blow slam into him between the shoulder blades. He felt himself hit the floor facedown, his back suddenly burning with pain. He rolled, but the kick caught him on the arm and sent him crashing into a trunk. He tried to roll again but there was no space and the huge hands closed around him, pulled him up, and lifted him into the air.

The giant flung him as though he were a doll, and he

smashed into the wall with a force that jarred every bone in his body. He dropped to the floor against the wall. He didn't try to meet the giant's next blow but catapulted himself forward. Igor, expecting him to try to cover up, had barreled forward, and Fargo heard his bellow of rage and pain as he smashed into the wall. Fargo fought away the pain of his own body as he rolled and pulled himself to his feet.

Another flash of lightning flooded the cellar for an instant, and Fargo saw the girl beside the stairs, her burning blue eyes fixed on the battle, her lips parted in excitement. Goddamn little bitch, Fargo swore silently as the surge of fury spiraled through him. The hulk raced toward him again and this time Fargo waited in a crouch, every muscle tensed. He measured distances and let the huge hands almost reach his throat. He dropped onto all fours, and Igor's tremendous bulk fell over him to crash to the floor. Fargo rose, leapt up into the air and came down with both feet on the giant's back.

Igor let out a roar of pain, and Fargo jumped to the side as the huge figure rolled over and started to pull himself to his feet. Fargo stared in astonishment as the giant rose up, towered into the air with his back plainly not broken. Igor dived forward, and Fargo threw a blazing right that connected with the man's jaw. The giant staggered, and Fargo delivered a whistling left cross, saw the brute leap into the air and his blow harmlessly bounce off the giant's chest. He tried to duck aside but Igor's mountainous form crashed down on him and he felt himself go down. Igor seized him from behind, lifted him again, and flung him in a sideways arc. Fargo landed half over a big, solid trunk and gasped out in pain.

He let himself go over the top and fell onto the other side of the trunk, a narrow space near the wall. He glimpsed the broken handle of a shovel on the floor, seized it, and swung from behind the trunk as the giant's treelike arms reached across for him. His blow caught the man along the side of the head, and Igor drew back in pain. He swung one tremendous arm in a backhand motion and smashed it against the broken shovel handle, and the weapon flew out of Fargo's hand. Fargo watched it skitter along the floor and he half-dived, half-leapt around the end of the trunk and fell on it, rolled, came up with the length of heavy wood again.

Igor charged—a rush worthy of a wounded buffalo—head down, massive bulk hurtling. Fargo swung his weapon in an upward arc. Igor glimpsed it and managed to twist his head, but the blow ripped up alongside his temple and a gush of blood erupted to run down the side of his head. Fargo ducked away from the giant, brought the length of wood crashing down on the shaven head. The broken handle splintered as it landed, and Igor went down. He dropped to both knees and hung there with his bleeding head moving from side to side, not unlike a grizzly gathering itself.

Fargo clasped both hands together, raised them over his head, and brought them down onto the back of Igor's neck with all his remaining strength. The hulk fell face forward onto the floor, lay there, a twitching mountain. He wasn't dead, only unconscious, his temple making a red puddle on the cellar floor. Fargo dropped to one knee to draw in deep, rasping breaths. He looked up to see the girl move toward him from the stairs, the rifle firmly pointed at him.

"Enjoy it, damn your hide?" Fargo gasped out between breaths.

"Yes," she said softly, excitement in the burning blue eyes, her lips slightly parted. "Very impressive. I've never seen anyone stand up to Igor, much less beat him."

"There's a first time for everything," Fargo spit out as he stayed on one knee and let his breath return.

"Too bad," the girl said, her pretty face expressionless.

"What's that mean?" Fargo growled.

"Too bad it was all for nothing," she said.

"All for nothing? Goddamn, I won. What the hell more do you want?" Fargo roared.

He saw her aim the rifle. "All for nothing," she repeated, and he dived, flung himself flat as he did so. "Goddamn bitch," he snarled as he hit the floor and felt the blast of rifle fire brush across his back. He rolled, scrambled for the corner where the Colt lay. He had almost reached it when her second shot rang out, and he felt the sharp, searing pain shoot through his head. He seemed on fire, a split-second burst of excruciating flame that vanished to leave nothing, neither pain nor sense nor feeling. The world ceased to exist.

Mists rose from the still waters to allow only a glimpse of trailing, tangled vines. Tall, knobby-kneed trees reached upward out of the watery depths to disappear into the mists, and long, sinuous tendrils hung down as if suspended in midair. Nothing seemed to move and yet there was life here, the air filled with a scent faintly musky yet sweet, hanging moss and mimosa, humus and hyacinth. In this place, it was as though time had stood still and a dark, deep silence seemed to own the world.

But something jarred this hanging quiet, something foreign disturbed its primeval beauty. Near the center of one watery passageway, an object lay against the roots of a bald cypress, more in the water than out. The object stirred, became a figure, shirt caught against the edge of a splintered knot in the tree trunk. It was the only thing that kept the figure's head out of the water as morning began to seep its way through the dense strands of hanging moss. Skye Fargo's eyelids twitched. It was the first sign of existence that he'd had since the rifle blast struck. He moved his eyelids again, forced them to pull open.

The effort sent waves of pain rushing through his head, and he lay still. But the pain refused to go away. He kept his eyes open, tried to focus, but he saw only formless areas of color as the pain throbbed through his head. He felt wetness, his body immersed in wetness, and he tried to think back. The rifle blast was all he could remember. There had been nothing after that. He forced himself to stare into space, and slowly the formless pieces of color began to take shape. He made out trees, water, long, hanging tendrils. The world began to reappear, and he glanced down to see his body almost completely submerged in the dull-green water.

He lifted his arm, stopped at once as the pain shot through his body. The faint movement sent water lapping against his face. He forced down the waves of pain to raise his head. He felt his shirt slip from the splintered piece of tree trunk that had held him. He reached up, almost cried out in pain, and caught hold of the knobby knees of the cypress that protruded from the water and held himself in place. He lowered his head as the pain swept through him.

The rifle blast had injured nerve endings that remained raw and throbbing, and Fargo clung to the perch and let the worst of the pain subside. He let his eyes take in the watery pathways that stretched out on both sides of him, the heavy tendrils hanging beside the moss. He espied a little island that rose up in the water, hardly more than a small mound of sago pondweed. It offered a refuge, a dry haven to rest. He couldn't cling much longer to the smooth tree root, he realized as he felt what little strength he had sliding out of his arms.

He half-turned, saw the dark-gray, knobby log lying mostly submerged in the water but near enough for him to easily reach. Another bumpy gray log lay three-quarters submerged a few yards farther on, and Fargo slowly let himself side completely into the water. He began to drift slowly. Suddenly, he froze as the nearest log blinked at him. He stared and the log blinked again, and he saw two tiny eyes protruding up in what he'd taken to be knobby, rough bark. The log moved, rose in the water, and at the end nearest him a row of jagged teeth appeared. Fargo swallowed as the log became a big, gray alligator, some twelve feet, he guessed, the bumpy gray bark its thick, warty hide.

Fargo's gasped curse lodged in his throat. He had slid from the smooth root of the cypress. He hadn't the strength to try to pull himself back. Besides, it would require too much effort and movement, and that, above all else, would be a fatal mistake. He floated on his back, arms pressed to his side, and tried to lie absolutely still in the water. He saw the other log rise and start to lazily move toward him. Letting only his eyes move, he watched the two alligators swim toward him, hardly rippling the water as they came. The pain still racked his body and his head. One snap of those crushing jaws could end it, but it wasn't a remedy he'd welcome. He watched the two gators half-turn with the barest movement of their tails. Both swam directly at him, their tiny eyes blinking.

Exciting Westerns by Jon Sharpe

Prices higher in Canada

**Buy them at your local
bookstore or use coupon
on next page for ordering.**

SIGNET Brand Westerns You'll Enjoy

$\mathcal{O}$ $\mathcal{C}$

More SIGNET and SIGNET CLASSIC Americana Novels

**Buy them at your local
bookstore or use coupon
on next page for ordering.**

Other Signet Westerns for you to enjoy